Kelly took a deep breath. *No time to worry about the track meet right now—time to concentrate on your acting. Get the right feeling, the right attitude.* "I've got it. I'm ready."

"Forget I'm here," Randy instructed from behind the camera. "Look right at the red light and your eyes will be focused in the right place. Can you remember that?"

"Yes, yes," she exclaimed. "Let's go!"

"Camera rolling."

She cocked her head to one side, flashed a high smile, and willed her eyes to light up with enthusiasm. "Balmour's has casuals," she began. Two-year-old Jessica hiccuped.

Cut!

I0639259

Kelly Blake
TEEN MODEL

One day she's an A student at Franklyn High with a major crush on the boy next door. Then she's discovered by the head of the prestigious FLASH! modelling agency. Almost overnight, Kelly becomes the hottest new face in the modelling world!

Each of the KELLY BLAKE titles features the ongoing characters and events in Kelly's life. While romance is part of that life, these books are more than romances; they deal with the experiences, conflicts, crises and behind-the-scenes details of modelling.

Ask your bookseller for the titles you have missed:

Coming soon:

•••••••• 3 •••••••••

KELLY BLAKE
TEEN MODEL

••••••••••••••••••••

Hard to Get

Yvonne Greene

BANTAM BOOKS
TORONTO • NEW YORK • LONDON • SYDNEY • AUCKLAND

**With special thanks to
Abby Daniels,
whose help was invaluable**

RL 6, IL age 12 and up

HARD TO GET
A Bantam Book / June 1987

*Setting of back-cover photo of Kelly Blake in the soda shoppe
courtesy of Antique Supermarket.*

ISBN 0-553-26087-5

*Bantam Books are published by Bantam Books, Inc. Its trade-
mark, consisting of the words "Bantam Books" and the portrayal
of a rooster, is Registered in U.S. Patent and Trademark Office
and in other countries. Marca Registrada, Bantam Books, Inc.,
666 Fifth Avenue, New York, New York 10103.*

*Reproduced, printed and bound in Great Britain by
Hazell Watson & Viney Limited,
Member of the BPCC Group,
Aylesbury, Bucks.*

Hard to Get

One

The doors marked Three Doves Production Company swung open, and Jennifer Lee, comfortably settled in a deep sofa in the reception area, saw her best friend, Kelly Blake, striding toward her. Kelly's curly golden brown hair bounced against her neck, and her blue-green eyes were bright. Her long skirt—its lines enhanced by her athletic stride—and the blouse casually belted around her hips revealed the sense of style Kelly had only recently developed. Kelly looked just the way she always did, yet something about her was very different.

Jennifer sprang off of the couch, knocking her computer textbook to the floor. "What happened? Are you all right? That took forever, I was getting worried."

Kelly smiled. "You are now, officially, the best friend of the new Balmour's Girl."

Jennifer screamed. "You got it! I don't believe it!" She grabbed Kelly's arms, and the two of them hugged and jumped up and down.

"Believe it," Kelly cried. "I beat everyone. I'm the new Balmour's Girl and I'm going to model clothes in all their television commercials for a year! An entire year, Jen!"

"I really can't believe it," Jennifer said again. "My best friend, on television. And the Balmour's Girl—that's a big deal, that's an exclusive contract for a famous store! This is the best thing that's ever happened to you!"

"It sure is. I never expected to get this part, Jen, I really didn't. Everyone warned me not to get my hopes up my first time auditioning for a part in a television commercial."

"*I'm* not surprised," Jennifer said loyally.

"And it even sounds like fun," Kelly exclaimed. "We're going to do a series of different life-style looks—a student, an athlete, and a baby-sitter. I hate the part of the baby-sitter, but naturally that's the spot we're going to shoot first."

"Spot . . . shoot . . . I love television talk," Jennifer sighed. "Welcome to show business, Kelly Blake. Well, it was only logical for them to choose you. You're fresh and almost an unknown, since you only started modeling this fall, and that means you'll be perfect for the Balmour's job."

"I don't think logic had anything to do with it. There were plenty of other 'fresh faces' auditioning today. I just got lucky, I guess. But I'm really worried about being a total beginner. The television people said I should be myself, but . . ."

Jennifer shook her head gently, her glossy black hair swinging across her shoulders. "Try saying 'production company,' not 'television people,'" she corrected Kelly. "Production companies produce television commercials—and Three Doves shoots some very important TV commercials."

"No matter what I call them, these television people don't realize what an amateur I am. Maybe they'll change their minds, back out before the contracts are signed." She shrugged. "Come on, let's go."

Jennifer rolled her eyes at her friend. "Kelly, you have everything it takes to be a top model, yet I'm still giving you pep talks before every big assignment. Where's your self-confidence?"

"Oh, it's there—buried under layers of confusion. Jen, I am doing the right thing, aren't I? I do want to be in this television commercial, don't I?"

Jennifer spoke patiently. "Kelly, we go through this every time you do something new. Last time it was the assignment to do that charity-ball fashion show, when you were terrified of falling off the runway. You never fell—in fact, you were the hit of the evening. The audience adored you, the press raved about you, and the designer asked you to model his next show!"

"But that was different." Kelly pushed the elevator button.

"How was it different? You were positive you'd be awful in the fashion show, and you ended up being the best. Just as you were sure you'd never make the track team at school, and you're Coach Hayes's most valuable new runner. With your record, you're almost guaranteed to be a movie star in a year."

"Do you really think so?" Sometimes, Kelly's new career seemed like a mistake, a dream—she couldn't possibly be the hottest new model with FLASH!, the top New York modeling agency. Yet she had a growing portfolio to prove it— pictures of herself posing in everything from swimsuits to glamorous evening gowns. Pictures that soon would be appearing in famous fashion magazines. It had happened so quickly, it seemed unreal. No wonder she fell apart before assignments.

She looked at her friend thoughtfully. "You know, Jen, more models should be like you— naturally neat, well organized, totally unfazed by things like auditions and strange places like production houses. I'm awfully glad I made you come with me today."

Jennifer gave a pleased smile. "That's what best friends are for. So tell me everything. Did they make you memorize your lines? What's the commercial about? What do you have to say?— tell me everything you remember."

"I don't have to tell you, I have the script right here." Kelly pulled the newly creased script out of her bag. "Start reading there, after the camera directions."

As Jennifer read, her expression changed from serious to disbelieving. Finally she started to laugh.

"What's so funny?"

"These lines—they're unbelievable! I know this isn't exactly drama, but still . . . I expected something else. You were so nervous about never acting before, but this is worse than any school play I've ever seen. It must be a joke."

"No, it's the real script, all right. I just hope I can do it justice."

"Do it justice?" Jennifer stared. "You've got to

be kidding. 'Balmour's means beautiful,'" she recited, suppressing a giggle. "That's the script? What are you worried about? Or how about this one, for the part of the student." She cleared her throat, assuming a haughty pose. " 'Balmour's junior separates and sportswear get top grades— Balmour's beats the competition!' "

"I know," Kelly said, "it sounds dumb when you read it like that. But in a real commercial it sounds much better. Look at my favorite part, the athlete."

" 'I carry the ball, but Balmour's carries the best. For casuals, sweats, and workout clothes, Balmour's makes your body talk!' " Jennifer laughed. "Kelly, what are you worried about? This isn't acting. All you have to do is spout a few silly slogans. And what terrible clichés."

"Well, I admit it's pretty stereotyped," Kelly agreed. "The student wears the coordinated outfit, the athlete wears sweatpants—"

"And the baby-sitter," Jennifer interrupted. "Naturally the baby-sitter is nervous because her boyfriend is coming over! Who wrote this stuff? Do they really think anyone talks this way: 'Balmour's has casuals for everybody's baby. Balmour's means beautiful—for any busy day!' "

"But it probably won't sound that bad when there are props around."

"I don't know, Kelly, maybe you could help them—maybe you could rewrite the lines, show them what *real* teenagers talk like."

"I hadn't thought about it, but maybe it's not such a bad idea." Kelly took the script. "You're so good at writing and stuff, Jen, maybe you should go into advertising. If you'd written this script, it would probably be much better."

"I'd do a whole documentary approach—you know, real kids in real situations, saying real things." Jennifer's dimples were showing as she added brightly, "But all of them would wear clothes from Balmour's Department Stores, of course."

"Naturally. What a scream—we could even have them film in Franklyn, at the high school."

"Perfect! You could use the track, and have Coach Hayes yelling at you, and"—Jennifer smiled wickedly—"good old Eric Powers waiting for you at the finish line. He could be the first prize."

Kelly flushed, as she always did whenever someone teased her about Eric. After months of suspense in which she'd wondered whether or not Eric was interested in her, Kelly's status as Eric's unofficial girlfriend was still new to her. When Eric finally admitted he was interested in Kelly— but that he wasn't free to date anyone exclusively because he had an agreement with a girl in his old hometown—Kelly had been so relieved that she happily became his sometime girl. Not that it was a perfect arrangement—far from it. But Kelly's modeling career was beginning to take up so much of her time, she wasn't sure she could handle a steady boyfriend, anyway.

"Hello," Jennifer called. "I lost you when I mentioned Eric's name. Come back, Kelly, wherever you are."

Kelly gave a short laugh. "Sorry. I got distracted."

"Eric is cute enough to distract anyone," Jennifer agreed.

The elevator finally came and they squeezed into the crowded car. In the lobby, Kelly nearly collided with a dark-haired girl coming out of a phone booth.

"Hey, watch out, I . . . Oh, hi, didn't I see you upstairs auditioning for the Balmour's spot? Wasn't it awful? It's always the same. Someday I'm going to get a real part on Broadway and forget all this crass commercial stuff. I wonder who got to be the stupid Balmour's Girl, anyway."

Kelly blushed, but Jennifer plunged right in. "She did," she said, pointing to Kelly. "She got the part."

"Oh, sorry. That's great." The girl shook Kelly's hand. "Congratulations." She patted Jennifer on the back. "You're a loser too, huh? Oh, well, join the club."

"Oh, no, I didn't audition," Jennifer explained. "I just came to keep Kelly company. I'm not a model."

"No? Could have fooled me. You exotic types are really popular nowadays."

Jennifer bristled. "I'm Chinese American, and that's not very exotic."

"Hey, don't take offense. I meant it as a compliment. You're very pretty, that's all I meant, and in this business every little extra counts. I mean, I'm a terrific actress, but I didn't get the part." She examined Kelly from head to toe. "I guess they like you athletic types whether you can act or not."

"They know I'm not an actress," Kelly said. "They didn't have to hire me. I auditioned like everyone else, and I must have been good or I wouldn't have gotten the job."

"Okay, maybe you're a natural, it happens. Listen, I'm sure you'll be great. I knew you were a model, though, because of your portfolio. I see you work for the FLASH! agency. I do some modeling, too, when I'm between acting gigs, which is most of the time. Maybe you've heard of me, Marty Tremaine? I wouldn't mind modeling for an agency like FLASH! Do you have any tips on how I could break in?"

Oh, no! Kelly thought, lowering her eyes. This wasn't the first time she'd been asked that question. Ever since she'd signed with FLASH!, it seemed everyone and their mothers knew someone who'd be the perfect model. It never helped when Kelly insisted there were no secrets to the job.

"Well"—she hesitated—"you apply to agencies, and go to interviews, and if you're what they want they hire you."

"That simple, huh?" Marty looked skeptical.

"It was for Kelly," Jennifer said. "She was discovered at a beauty make-over, by Meg Dorian herself, the head of FLASH!"

"Jen," Kelly said quietly. Jennifer had no idea how envious and jealous some girls could get over Kelly's success story. Sometimes people's reactions made Kelly uncomfortable. "That isn't the usual way."

"I'm afraid that will never happen to me," Marty said mournfully. "I'm more of a character actress, and I don't have the right looks for big-time modeling."

"No, really, you're very attractive," Kelly insisted.

Marty gave a hopeful smile. "Then could you kind of show me around at FLASH!—introduce me to Meg Dorian, maybe?"

Kelly squirmed. Just what she'd been dreading! "I don't know, I'm not there that often," she said vaguely. "Anyway, you should have comps made, you know—eight-by-ten glossies, with several poses—"

"Those are expensive!" Marty cried. "Forget it. I thought you'd have some real insider's tips. I'm sorry I asked. Well, good luck and see you at the movies."

"Do you really think she could model for FLASH!?" Jennifer said as Marty bounded across the lobby.

"Truthfully?" Kelly shook her head. "No way. Not that she isn't interesting looking, but she'd have to find an agency that liked her particular face. Even today, when there are so many ways to look, you still have to have a certain something that Marty doesn't have."

"And besides that?"

Kelly sighed. "Besides that, she doesn't take it seriously enough. Sure, good photos are expensive, but you've simply got to have them. Modeling is a tough business. Marty doesn't act at all professional about it." She hesitated, then confessed to Jennifer, "If Marty and I were up for the same modeling job, I could get it in a second because I know how to behave on interviews."

Jennifer nodded. "I see what you mean," she said. "You're pretty smart about this business, Kelly." She followed her friend into the revolving glass door.

"I've learned to be smart about it," Kelly continued when they were both outside. They began to walk toward the Port Authority Bus Terminal. "In my reading, for instance, I was definitely miscast as the baby-sitter, but I gave it my best effort, and I was the baby-sitter to end all baby-sitters."

She grasped Jennifer. "Hey, what if Marty's right? What if I have a natural dramatic ability I didn't know about before? I can't wait to see where my career goes next—maybe I'll get a part in a TV series."

"Dramatic ability?" Jennifer grinned crookedly. "No offense, but a commercial isn't a TV series. Aren't you getting a little carried away with this?"

"Carried away? No, you heard Marty—I must have *some* genuine acting talent. There were plenty of pretty girls in there, Jen, and they didn't get the part."

"But, Kelly, I thought we agreed those lines were a joke. 'Balmour's has casuals for everybody's baby'—it should be Balmour's has contempt for anybody's baby—anybody who would buy their overpriced clothes."

"It may not be the best script in the world, but that's the whole point—it isn't easy to make stiff dialogue sound natural, and to smile and project the idea of the Balmour's Girl at the same time takes real ability. Acting is a skill, you know, it does involve technique."

"What kind of technique do you have? You never acted before in your life, not even in grade school when we did a class play every year. You were always glad to be in the background then. You used to be more . . . modest."

"I'm not trying to act conceited, Jennifer. But there's nothing wrong with recognizing your own talents. How do you think I get a modeling assignment? Do you think I walk into an interview and say, 'Oh gee, I'm no good, I'm only average, don't hire me'?"

"Kelly," Jennifer moaned.

"That's all I mean when I say I'm good. I'm just being an objective professional. I'm not bragging."

"Sounds like bragging to me," Jennifer muttered.

Kelly didn't hear her. She was busy leafing through her copy of the script. "You know, I was a pretty shy kid most of my life," she said. "But lots of actors are shy. They say introverts make the best actors, because they're able to jump into another person's skin. Shy people are very observant, very sensitive."

"Hummmph."

"I was always so self-conscious, remember, Jen? So tall and skinny and awkward. Being a model has really helped me—I'm much more self-confident now. Imagine, I could actually become a movie star because of all this. I wonder if I should change my name? 'Starring Kelly Blake' . . . too ordinary, don't you think?"

"Maybe it is," Jennifer said impatiently. "And maybe I should start auditioning, like Marty said. Five foot four is too short to model, but you don't have to be tall to be an actress, and after all, I *am* the exotic type."

"Come on, Jen, you could never bare your soul in front of strangers. Especially not producers and directors like I met at my audition—they're the type you always make fun of." She shuddered, imagining how her friend would behave. "You'd probably tell them to their faces that they're shallow, disgusting people." Kelly laughed heartily.

"I don't see why you're saying that. I could get

a part, too, if I wanted one. I can be as competitive as you when I have to."

"Sure—at winning scholarships. Anyway, I can't wait to tell everyone at school about this. Seriously, Jen, even though I gave a good reading, do you think I'll do a good job when it's for real?"

"Just rely on your natural acting talent."

Kelly missed the sarcasm in Jennifer's voice. "Do you think that's enough? Maybe I'd better start acting lessons."

"Oh, sure. Why don't you start them tonight?"

"Tonight! I almost forgot. I have a date with Eric tonight!"

"Your mom let you make a date for a school night?"

"Yes, because Eric and his family are flying to Ohio on Friday night, so we couldn't see each other over the weekend. I've been working so hard she thought I deserved a special treat. I have to work late on Friday, too."

Jennifer looked astounded. "Ohio—where Eric used to live?"

"Yellow Springs, Ohio," Kelly said, trying to sound nonchalant. "His old hometown. They're going to visit their friends and family there."

"You're not worried about Eric getting together with his old girlfriend?" Jennifer said. "Sounds dangerous to me."

"I'm a little worried." Kelly shrugged. "But I can't stop Eric from seeing Clarissa if he wants to. After all, we made an agreement that we're both free to date other people. Don't I date Alex Hawkins, too?"

"I guess. I wish I had your problems—two

boys to choose from. I'd take Eric in a minute, if I had to choose."

Kelly shook her head. "It's not that easy. I like each of them for different reasons. I can hardly believe Eric and I finally got together. I thought I'd spend my life just dreaming about him. He's so sweet, but so shy, sometimes I hardly feel that I've gotten to know him. Whereas Alex—he's so up-front, sometimes it scares me. He just lays everything right on the line. He likes me and he tells me so."

"And he's handsome and rich. That doesn't hurt," Jennifer said.

"And interesting," Kelly added. "He's friendly with all kinds of people, and he takes me to terrific places, like that nightclub we went to on our second date. Alex knew the club owner, and we got special seats for the floor show. Eric wouldn't take me to a nightclub even if he could afford it. He'd probably take me on a bike ride and a picnic instead. But I like doing those things, too. I guess I'm just lucky I don't have to choose between them."

"Well, you'd better watch out," Jennifer warned. "Dating two boys is playing with fire. Unless, of course, Eric keeps on dating other girls from Franklyn. Then it would have to be okay for you to date other guys too."

"*Keeps* dating . . . What do you mean?"

"I didn't tell you this before," Jennifer said hesitantly, "but now I think you ought to know."

"Know what?"

"Eric took Shana Brody to the disco last weekend, when you were doing that *Jolie* magazine job. I saw them there."

Kelly was shocked. "You told me he wasn't with anyone special."

"I thought it would bother you, but maybe it's best if you know everything."

"But, Shana . . ." Kelly thought of Shana's flashy clothes, her trendy haircut, and her over-done makeup. "She's hardly his type."

"It probably didn't mean anything," Jennifer said. "I went with Jason Barry and that didn't mean anything—it was just friendly, that's all."

Kelly gave a sickly grin, her successful audition completely forgotten.

"Maybe I shouldn't have said anything." Jennifer looked contrite. "I'm sure they're just friends, Kelly. Forget I told you—Eric obviously likes you. Besides, he's usually too busy working out or fixing that old car of his to see anybody. And worrying about who else he's going out with will only make you uncomfortable around him."

"Ugh. How do things get so complicated? But you're probably right. Okay, I'll just try not to think about it."

It wasn't until they were safely on the bus to New Jersey, the New York skyline disappearing from view, that Kelly found herself wondering why Jennifer had told her anything at all about Eric and Shana Brody. It almost seemed as if Jennifer had told her out of spite. But *that's ridiculous*, she told herself. *Jennifer is my best friend. She'd never do anything like that.*

Two

Kelly's mother was putting the finishing touches on her famous roast chicken when Kelly burst into the kitchen.

"Roast chicken—my favorite," Kelly cried in dismay. "Why did you have to make it tonight, when you know I'm going out to eat?"

"Honey, the rest of us have to eat, too," Judith Blake said. She lifted the chicken carefully from the roasting pan to a carving board. "Close the oven door, will you, Kelly?"

"Promise you'll save me some."

Her mother nodded and picked up a towel to wipe off her hands. "Well—how did it go?"

"I got it," Kelly said proudly.

"Does that mean you're the new Balmour's Girl?"

"Yes, and they made up their minds right away. I beat dozens of other girls."

"Why, that's great," her mother said proudly. "That's terrific! Dad will be thrilled—this is big news."

"I know. I'll have to study my script, but there aren't very many lines. Oh, are my jeans ironed? I need them for tonight."

"I can't believe you're worried about your jeans at a time like this. Tina's upstairs—why don't you go tell her your good news. And why don't you dress up a little more for your date tonight?"

"I don't want to dress up. Did Eric call?"

Mrs. Blake began rinsing off the lettuce for that night's salad. "He did—about an hour ago. He's *so* polite . . ."

"Am I supposed to call him back or what?"

"No, he didn't say you should call."

Kelly hurried up the stairs to her room to change. She was running a little late, so if Eric didn't call again while she was getting dressed, she'd just run over and get him. That was the nicest thing about their relationship, the fact that they were friends and could be casual with each other.

Not that Kelly felt completely casual as she crossed the street to Eric's house. She ran her fingers through her hair hurriedly before ringing the doorbell, and reached inside her jacket to tighten the belt around her hips, straightening her shirt carefully.

No one answered the bell. She tried the front door, but it was locked. Then she noticed that Eric's car wasn't in the driveway where it usually was.

"Hello. . . . Anybody home? Eric?" Pressing her face against the living room window, she peered inside, but curtains covered the windows and it was difficult to see clearly. "Eric!" she called again. "Hello. . . . Anybody . . ."

"In the garage," she heard Eric's voice call. She stepped off the porch and hurried around the side of the house to the garage, where she found both Eric and his car.

"Oh, no. What happened?"

"Didn't you get my message?" Eric pushed himself out from under his car on a small wooden board with wheels.

"What message?" Kelly's heart sank. "I just know you called."

He sat up, brushing at the grime on his shirt. "Sorry—maybe I wasn't clear enough. I have car trouble."

"That's obvious."

"I guess your Mom didn't understand my message. I meant that I'd have to cancel tonight. It's my fault—I should have been more specific, but I was kind of flipped out about the carburetor. I'm really sorry, Kelly."

She didn't know what to say. She'd been looking forward to their date, and there wasn't any other night that week that she could see him.

"I should've called," she mumbled, embarrassed that she had barged right over, expecting that Eric would be thrilled to see her. "No one answered the door."

"Yeah, my folks are out and my brother Timmy's at a friend's. That's why I canceled—I couldn't even borrow my parents' car." He shrugged helplessly. "I'm stuck here."

"It's okay." The thought that now she could have her mother's roast chicken for dinner after all didn't cheer her up in the least. She didn't even have much of an appetite.

"I don't mind too much. Anyway, I had a great day today."

"Oh, your audition— was it good?" he asked.

"It was great. I got the job." Eric had never seemed impressed by her career, so she downplayed its importance to her when they were together.

"Hey, congratulations. Oh—" He looked crestfallen. "Now we should be celebrating together, instead of canceling our date. I'm sorry, Kelly. I'll make it up to you sometime, I promise." Eric stared at his grease-stained clothes and hands. "I guess I'll grab some peanut butter and jelly and clean this carburetor down in the cellar."

Kelly made a face. "Peanut butter—can't you do better than that? Maybe you could eat with my family, or . . ." She had a sudden inspiration. "Does your mom have any spaghetti in the house?"

"I guess so."

"I can cook a great spaghetti dinner! I could make dinner for the two of us . . . unless you'd rather work on the car."

Eric smiled. "That's a great idea—we can cook it together! It's not the date I had in mind, but . . . I'll just grab a shower. You don't mind waiting, do you?"

"If you're sure you wouldn't rather clean the carburetor."

"Who needs it?" Eric threw his tools into a pile on the garage floor. "You're a great sport—after all, I promised to buy you dinner, not force you to cook it."

Kelly grinned. "This will be more fun. I'll poke around to see what kind of groceries you have in the house."

Eric let them in the back door. "Uh . . . I'm not sure I know where everything is."

"No problem. I'll find what I need."

"You're in charge," he said with a grin. "But try to keep the explosions to a minimum, okay?"

"I'll have everything started by the time you get cleaned up," she boasted.

"Yes, dear." Imitating a dutiful husband, Eric leaned over and kissed her on the cheek.

"And don't forget to shave," she added. He snapped his jacket at her playfully.

While she worked, Kelly pretended that she and Eric were in *their* house, she was in *their* kitchen, following her usual weeknight routine. In no time, she had everything organized for their dinner. Upstairs, she could hear faint sounds of Eric's whistling in the shower. It gave her a warm, cozy feeling.

By the time Eric came bounding downstairs, she had a pot of water boiling on the stove, sauce simmering on a back burner, and fresh vegetables set out, ready to be quickly steamed when the spaghetti was just about done. The special treat was her own favorite, garlic bread. There hadn't been any fresh Italian bread in the house, so she'd split a couple of long rolls meant for sub sandwiches. Then she'd poured a mixture of sautéed garlic and melted butter over them before setting them in the oven to get crisp and brown on top.

She hurried into the dining room, a filled wineglass in each hand.

"What's the matter?" she said.

Eric was staring at the table, open mouthed.

"I can't believe what you did," he said in

delight. Lighted candles glowed on the dining room table, which was covered with a soft blue tablecloth and decorated with an arrangement of blue and white silk flowers that Kelly had found in the living room.

"It looks beautiful," he said.

Kelly set the glasses down and sat at the head of the table. "I'm glad you like it."

Eric pulled out the chair to her right and sat, lifting his wineglass. "A toast," he said dramatically, "to the perfect hostess."

They clinked glasses.

"Hey—this is Coke," he sputtered.

"I couldn't find anything else except cooking sherry," she explained with a laugh.

"Well, it's my favorite year for Coke." With a flourish, Eric drained the glass. "My compliments to the chef," he said.

"The chef didn't make the wine."

"Then my compliments to whoever made the chef," he teased, leaning closer. She lowered her glass to the tabletop, expecting to be kissed. Eric hesitated, and she hesitated, too—was he going to kiss her or not? Kelly leaned forward decisively and kissed Eric.

So what if she kissed him first, as long as he returned the kiss with plenty of enthusiasm. Sometimes he was too shy for his own good. Suddenly there was a loud, horrible buzz.

"What's that?" she cried, and they pulled apart, jumping guiltily.

"The kitchen timer," Eric explained. They burst out laughing.

"Time to rescue the pasta," Kelly said.

As they ate, Eric told her stories of disasters he'd had with his car.

She laughed so hard that she begged him to stop. "My side hurts," she complained, wiping her eyes with the back of her hand.

"I'll stop—if you promise to put my carburetor back together."

"I don't know anything about cars," Kelly protested. "At least, not their insides. I only know whether or not they look good."

"Speaking of good-looking cars," Eric said casually, "that's a nice sports car, that 300ZX I've seen you in."

Alex's car! Kelly hadn't told Eric anything about Alex.

"That belongs to someone I work with, a photographer's assistant," she said, but she flushed. *What if Eric saw Alex kiss me good night? What if Eric knows I'm lying, knows that Alex is more than someone I work with?*

"Hey, forget I mentioned it." Eric dug into the last piece of garlic bread.

She frowned. "What if it was someone I've started dating. Is there anything wrong with that?"

"I didn't say—"

"You and I don't have any agreements—you're the one who wants to keep it light, because of—of what's-her-name!"

"I'm not trying to start a fight," Eric said.

"Then why were you spying on me, anyway?" Kelly demanded.

"I never spied on you. . . . I just happened to notice that car around here a couple of times. It's sort of hard to miss—especially when whoever owns it drives like a maniac."

"Alex is a very good driver. He's older than us—in college."

"Alex, huh?" Eric was silent. "Look," he finally said, "I explained to you about Rissa. Our parents are friends—and besides, she depends on me."

"She uses you." Moodily, Kelly pushed the remnants of her meal around on her plate. It was useless to get upset about Rissa after practically admitting she'd been dating Alex. But the mere mention of Rissa's name gave her a sinking feeling in her stomach.

"Believe me, I'm not jealous," she insisted. "You're free to do what you want." It was all so confusing. Maybe if Eric didn't have a Rissa, she wouldn't have an Alex. Maybe she could get closer to Eric if she didn't feel someone else was in the way.

Eric squirmed uncomfortably. "There's nothing I can do about it."

"Don't go to Ohio," she said flippantly.

"It's not that easy—I can't stay away when my family goes to visit. And Rissa's older brother is one of my best friends."

The mention of Rissa and Alex had cast a pall over their perfect evening. Dully, Kelly began to clear the table, and Eric scraped the dishes and loaded them into the dishwasher.

Oh, well, she thought, *at least Rissa never comes to visit Eric in Franklyn—that would be simply awful.* She'd die if that ever happened. At least this way, Eric kept the two of them separate. And no one in Franklyn (besides Kelly and Jennifer) had any idea that Eric kept in touch with his old girlfriend.

"Let's play some records," Eric suggested when the last of the dishes were in the dishwasher.

He turned on the stereo, and Kelly threw herself into the music, dancing more freely than she ever had before. After a few fast numbers, a slow song played, and she found herself in Eric's arms.

It was torture. If only Rissa didn't exist! If only Rissa hadn't known Eric first, hadn't slow-danced with him, kissed him . . .

It hurts. It really hurts. But I can't let Eric know. I'm a good actress, I found that out today. I just won't let Eric see how jealous I am of Rissa and Shana . . . of anyone who gets to be with him. I'll be light and fun to be with, and compared to me, Clarissa will seem like a total bore. And it won't hurt any if Eric is jealous of Alex. He'll see what he's missing, and he'll realize he likes me best. I know he will.

Kelly pulled out of Eric's arms, leaning back to look at his face. "Let's put some fast music back on," she suggested. "I have a new step to try out."

Prissy Rissy, watch out—you won't stand a chance. I'll be the kind of girl Eric really wants—or I don't know Eric Powers!

They danced for another hour, until they both were exhausted and were glad to collapse onto the living room couch. Eric reached over, brushing damp hair out of Kelly's eyes. How easy it would be to kiss him again, to lean against him flirtatiously. . . . But that wasn't the way she wanted to win Eric. *Let him pursue you. Get him interested*, Kelly told herself—*play a little hard to get.*

"It's late," she said, hunting for her jacket and pocketbook.

"Don't go . . ." Eric held out a hand.

But it was too hard to stay with Eric, knowing Rissa still had a claim on him.

She put her jacket over her shoulders and opened the door. "See you in school," she called out as she ran across the street.

At the last minute, before closing her own front door, Kelly turned around. Eric was standing in his doorway, watching her.

So far so good. Kelly waved—then, firmly, she closed the door.

Three

Jennifer waved from across the cafeteria. "Over here, Kelly. I got a table in the corner where no one will bother us."

Kelly dumped her books on the table. "Phew, it feels great to sit down. I can't believe this day. Everyone's heard about the commercial, and I haven't had a moment to myself. I think everyone in the entire school wants to talk to me about it. It's tough being a star."

"I'll bet. Well, here's the chapter I told you about." Jennifer laid her computer-programming text on the table between them.

"Wait a minute—there's Lisa and Rochelle. Why don't we go sit with them?"

"Remember, I have to cram for my computer-programming test. You promised to help during lunch."

"Oh, that's right. Well, just let me get some of this sandwich down before I faint from hunger."

Jennifer scribbled down a sample question for Kelly to ask. "Here, Kelly, I . . . Oh, look out—it's Julie Higgins and Patty Berg, coming this way. What could they want?"

Kelly peered across the room, trying not to be too obvious. "Since when do we rate? The two of them don't usually go out of their way to talk to us."

Julie rushed toward their table. "Heard about your new job, Kelly. How exciting! You must be thrilled that they chose you."

"I am," Kelly said warily. "It should be a lot of fun."

"Fun—it's an honor! You'll be famous soon, and rich. Listen, I have a favor to ask you."

"Me?" Kelly exchanged a suspicious glance with Jennifer. "What kind of favor?"

"I was hoping you'd be willing to speak to the Drama Club about your experience. Everyone would love to know how to become a TV actress. You could explain how to audition for commercials—it's such a big field these days."

"I don't know, Julie, I'm pretty new at it."

"Well, we could discuss it at my party tonight." Julie smiled brightly at Kelly, and Jennifer turned back to her book, pretending not to notice that she hadn't been invited.

"I have a modeling job tonight," Kelly explained. "It's a rush job for a big catalog and I'll be working pretty late. Thanks, anyway."

"No problem." Julie put her hand on Kelly's arm. "I'd love you to come, but we can still do the Drama Club project. I'll take care of all the details myself. You'll just have to show up.

Everyone's dying to hear you. You wouldn't disappoint them, would you?"

"I guess not," Kelly replied. "When will it be?"

"A week from Monday, I think. That should give me time to get everything organized."

"It will be just the Drama Club, won't it?"

"And anyone else who's interested, and I'm pretty sure plenty of kids will be interested. So, can I count on you?"

"Sure."

Julie squeezed Kelly's arm lightly, and Patty flashed her best cheerleader smile. "I knew you'd do it. You have a lot of school spirit, and I admire that. See you later."

Jennifer snorted. "Can you believe that? She probably wants it on her college applications that she organized a big club event."

"It's just the Drama Club," Kelly protested. "There probably won't be more than ten or twelve kids there. It will be kind of fun, me being an expert at something for a change."

"You don't need Patty Berg or Julie Higgins buttering you up. I thought you said they were the biggest snobs on the face of the earth and you would never be in their crowd."

"This has nothing to do with anybody's crowd. I'm not exactly best friends with the girl, I'm just doing her a favor. Do you have something against the Drama Club?"

"No."

"Then what's the big deal?"

"I just think it's slightly strange that you're willing to be so buddy-buddy with the golden girls all of a sudden."

"Jennifer, if I was rude to them I'd be acting just as snobby as they do. Let's drop it, okay? I'm too starved to argue. Give me your textbook. What's this mean—Entry Parameters to set I/O Byte?"

"That's the part I'm having trouble with, operating system call conventions."

"Okay, I'll ask you these questions. Oh, wait a minute, Patty is motioning me over to her table. I'll just be a minute, okay?"

Across the room, Patty and Julie moved over, making room for Kelly at their table among a group of laughing girls.

"You forgot your sandwich," Jennifer said wryly.

Four

Kelly stretched out her cramped right leg. Next to her on the beach blanket, Paisley Gregg stifled a yawn and rolled over, pretending to be sunbathing under the artificial glare of the spotlights that filled Steve Hollender's studio.

"If you close your eyes," Paisley said, "you can almost believe we're at the beach instead of working a catalog shoot. It's nearly as boring."

"Stop complaining and listen to me," Kelly said. "The audition was humiliating at first. They treated us like cattle—marched us in and out and asked dumb questions and didn't listen to the answers—and they were insulting." She shuddered. "I felt like an insect or something. As if they didn't care about *me* at all—like I could be replaced by any other girl instantly. It was all I could do to give a good reading."

Paisley stared at her coolly. "What did you

expect? To be treated like Kate Hepburn? It's no different from modeling—you should know better by now."

"Come on, this was much harder than modeling! I'm just glad I impressed them after all."

Paisley shrugged indifferently. "There are people who treat even top models like numbers," she said.

"Maybe, but when you model no one makes fun of the way you talk," Kelly pointed out. "And you don't have to worry about where to put your hands while you're saying your lines, or how to act like someone's idea of a bubbly teenager. Acting is much more demanding than straight modeling, and you know it."

Paisley drummed her fingers impatiently. "Okay, okay. Of course it's hard. If it was easy anybody could do it. That was the whole point of the audition, wasn't it? You have to be special to be the Balmour's Girl. So don't try to impress me. I wish I'd gotten a chance to be the Balmour's Girl. It's *fantastic* exposure, and when your contract is up, you get a *million* other offers. I'd give anything for a chance like that! But Meg would never send me to that audition—no one wants this Southern accent of mine on Yankee television."

"I think it's your coloring," Kelly said honestly. "There aren't too many girls with bright red hair and black eyes, and I think they want a model everyone can identify with. And besides, you don't always have a Southern accent. I've heard you speak without it."

Paisley drew away as if stung. "I *always* have a Southern accent," she drawled thickly.

"Okay, okay," Kelly quickly agreed. "You always do. Anyway, you would have hated the script. Even I could have written better copy."

"Sure you could. You could be a model, an actress, and an advertising copywriter." Paisley lifted her eyebrows scornfully.

"Even Jennifer says the lines are stupid. I'm telling you, Paisley, it isn't easy to act with such bad material."

"Jennifer!" Paisley scoffed. "Jennifer doesn't know anything about TV commercials. She isn't even a professional. Who cares what Jennifer thinks!" She narrowed her eyes. "What was she doing there, anyway?"

Kelly flushed. "She . . . wanted to come along," she lied.

Paisley shook her head, giving Kelly a pitying look. "You brought your *girlfriend* to an audition? You're lucky they didn't kick you out—how immature! Do you also suck your thumb? Are you afraid of the dark . . ."

"Cut it out," Kelly complained. "There's nothing wrong with having a best friend who wants to help you out."

"Honey," Paisley drawled, "there's *everything* wrong with having a best friend tag along on assignments. Do you want people to treat you like a little baby? Grow up, girl!"

Since Paisley was only a year older than Kelly was, Kelly found this advice rather insulting. "If you had a friend to bring along, you would," she said.

Paisley winced; the remark had hit closer to the truth than Kelly realized.

"Hey, Paisley—I'm sorry, I didn't mean that. . . ."

"Oh, it probably doesn't matter who went with

you," Paisley said calmly, refusing, as always, to discuss her personal life. "Kelly Blake can do no wrong. It's positively *sickening* how everyone falls for that wholesome act of yours. Like him—" Paisley nodded toward Alex, who was busy taking light-meter readings on the set.

"Twenty-two eight," Alex announced as he held the light meter next to Margaretta, the third model on the set. A flash went off.

"Twenty-two seven," Alex said this time. Margaretta, a buxom redhead, yawned as the light flashed again. "Thirty-two three—way too hot!"

"Let's get it down," Steve Hollender called. He was balanced at the top of a ladder, his head brushing the ceiling of the studio. Beside him, the camera was mounted on a tall tripod that looked like a black lamppost. The unusual shooting angle was necessary because the layout for the exclusive Butterfly catalog called for a full view of the three models, Kelly, Paisley, and Margaretta, posing on beach towels to show off the newest swimsuits.

"It's a good thing it takes so long to set the lights," Kelly said to change the subject. "It gives us a chance to talk. You're never home at night when I call you."

"True. An active social life is one of the fringe benefits of modeling." Paisley stretched, then rested comfortably on her side as Alex held the light meter next to her skin. A flash went off.

"Twenty-two six," Alex called.

"Great," Steve said. "I'll do a Polaroid."

"I'll bet you never knew modeling was going to involve so much waiting around." Paisley sighed. "I'm so used to doing fashion spreads—moving all the time while they zip off two dozen shots with those automatic cameras. Catalogs really are boring, holding these long poses while Steve lines us up to fit some art director's layout."

Margaretta, lying behind Paisley, stared over at Kelly jealously. "I heard you were getting to be a big shot at FLASH!," she said. "But I didn't know you thought catalog shoots were beneath you."

"I didn't say that," Kelly protested, but Margaretta snorted.

"Oh, yeah? Miss Cover Girl, complaining about holding still for five minutes at a time. We all should have it so tough. I suppose if you get to do the TV commercial you're constantly talking about, you'll be even more insufferable."

"Hey, I never put down catalog work," Kelly said, but Paisley gripped her arm, motioning for her to calm down.

"Save your breath," she said in a low voice. "Some girls are just the jealous type. Margaretta can't hurt your career, and she can't help it either. Ignore her."

High atop his ladder, Steve frowned at the girls. "Enough gabbing, get back into the pose. Margaretta, that's nice, really good. Hold that position."

Paisley nudged Kelly with her elbow, smirking at Margaretta's suggestive pose.

"That's very good, Margaretta. Uh, Kelly— this is a bathing suit ad, you know. I mean, let's see some cleavage. Your body's going to sell the suit."

Kelly glanced at Margaretta's lush body and then down at her own chest—not exactly the kind of cleavage men went wild over. Still, hardly any models she knew had the figure Margaretta had.

She (and Paisley, too, for that matter) had more of a dancer's body, slim and firm-muscled and athletic.

"Psst . . ." Paisley nudged her again. "Do this," she whispered, showing Kelly how to push one arm against her side so that her breasts seemed to bulge in the low-cut swimsuit.

"I *am* doing that," Kelly hissed. "There's only so much raw material to work with."

Steve nodded. "Better. . . . Let's get more of an angle, pull your arm down, Kelly, come on. You've got to sell your body."

Kelly blushed furiously, and Margaretta cackled, loving every second of Kelly's discomfort. "How long do you expect to be a model, Kelly? Until full-length swimsuits come back in style?"

Kelly couldn't help glancing at Alex, who was politely standing by, careful to keep all expression off his face. To her surprise, Kelly felt a burst of vanity. She had a nice body, too. She just didn't show it off to anyone and everyone like some people did.

From behind her Paisley whispered, "Give them more than that. What are you worried about? Steve would love it if we were all stark naked, and Alex doesn't care—he's been around models longer than you have. Believe me, he's seen it all."

"He hasn't seen all of me," Kelly muttered under her breath.

"Oh, come on, girl." Margaretta reached out and snapped Kelly's swimsuit strap, threatening to expose Kelly's breast completely.

"Margaretta!" Kelly yanked her suit up, blushing furiously. Luckily Alex seemed to be looking the other way. "You're not funny. Just leave me alone, okay? I don't need your help."

"Relax." Paisley laughed. "She didn't mean anything. Anyway, what's the big deal? Alex has seen it all before, hasn't he?"

"No," Kelly cried indignantly, "why would he?"

"Well," Paisley said in honest surprise, "well, for one thing, I thought you were dating."

"What if we are? Does that mean I went that far with him?"

"Why not?"

"Paisley, you're too much! I don't believe you're half as wild as you pretend to be. And as for Alex and me, we're just good friends."

"Then you're crazy. What are you holding back for? Alex Hawkins may be the catch of the century! He's rich and gorgeous and his father is a big wheel in the fashion industry. What more do you want? For Pete's sake, don't play hard to get with him."

"I'm not playing hard to get."

Paisley shook Kelly's arm. "Wake up, Kelly! Alex is a real catch. You're lucky you've got him interested. So don't lose him by being a prude."

"Wait a minute—I do like Alex, but we're not about to have the romance of the century. I'm involved with someone else, and you know it."

"I know—dear old Eric Powers." Paisley rolled her eyes. "It's beyond me how you could let a nobody like Eric stand between you and Alex."

"You've never even met Eric, so don't knock him."

"Honey, I don't have to meet him. For one thing, he's a lost cause. Eric *has* a girlfriend, right? And anyway, he's *young*—a high-school boy! He's not at all sophisticated or worldly, and he doesn't know anything about film or art or music—things you need to know about to get into the right circles."

"I'm not trying to get into *any* circle," Kelly protested. "I enjoy learning about those things when I'm with Alex, but Eric and I have so much more in common! We're both athletic; we come from the same kind of families, even the same neighborhood. We're so much alike that I don't have to think twice when I'm with him. I'm never nervous or worried about what to say or how to act. How do I explain to you . . . Eric is, he's . . ."

"I know," Paisley sighed, "he's comfortable—like an old shoe."

"It's not that at all. But having a lot in common makes it easier to . . . to communicate with him."

Paisley made an impatient face. "Any girl in her right mind would choose Alex over Eric. Even if he weren't fabulously wealthy, just look at him—he's gorgeous!" She narrowed her eyes suspiciously. "You're not obligated to Eric in any way, are you? You're not stupid enough to get secretly engaged or anything?"

"Of course not." Kelly watched as Alex taped a backdrop onto a stand with quick, assured movements. Alex was thin and wiry, while Eric's build was athletic, sturdy, almost rugged. Eric had the kind of half-man-half-little-boy looks that all the girls at Franklyn High adored. *Cute* was the word they used to describe Eric.

Alex, on the other hand, was definitely handsome; finely cut features, curly blond hair, soft gray eyes—in fact, Alex had the same breezy good looks as the male models Kelly worked with.

"Don't worry, I'm not secretly engaged to Eric or anything like that. It's just easier for me to be with Eric than Alex. Maybe it's because Alex is rich. He's always had everything easy. Maybe I don't know how to relate to that."

"I think you're afraid."

"Afraid of Alex? I am not."

"No, afraid of growing up. Eric is easy, you're the old Kelly Blake with him—just a high-school kid. But with Alex it's different. He's been around and he expects more from you. You have to work harder to keep up with Alex. *That's* what's wrong with him—you're intimidated by Alex."

"I am not," Kelly insisted.

"Good. Because Alex is rich, he's fun to be with, he'd take you anywhere and buy you anything," Paisley pointed out, "and don't forget—he's well connected. And if you want to make it in this business, and, say, sell your name for your own line of clothes like I want to do someday—it doesn't hurt to have people like Alex and his father on your side."

"I don't want to use Alex," Kelly protested.

Paisley groaned. "Oh, why do I even bother? Can't you see I'm trying to help you?"

"Look, Paisley, I like things the way they are, okay? Alex is a friend and a casual date and that's fine."

"Oh, have it your way. I suppose you have a hot date lined up with Eric tonight. Where are you going—bowling and then necking in the parking lot?"

"Cut it out," Kelly almost shouted. "If you must know, Eric is on his way to Ohio right now."

"Perfect! Then ask Alex out tonight," Paisley said immediately. "It's great timing, you're lucky. Just suggest you two grab a bite together after the shoot. You can handle that, can't you?"

"Paisley," Kelly said, losing all patience, "that's not the point—"

"Watch out!" Steve yelled.

Kelly flinched instinctively as a spotlight crashed to its side on the floor beside her, missing her by inches.

"Kelly, are you okay?" In an instant, Alex was kneeling beside her to see if she'd been burned.

"I'm fine—but I didn't even see it coming," she said shakily.

"Is anyone hurt?" Steve called.

"She's all right," Alex told him. He put a steadying arm around Kelly's shoulder.

Steve glared down at them. "Lucky for you— my insurance premiums are high enough as it is! Try to be more careful down there."

Kelly and Alex exchanged a quick glance. It was really no one's fault—the studio was so crowded, someone was bound to knock into something sometime.

"Insurance," Alex muttered to Kelly. "It's you he ought to be worried about." Their eyes locked, and something about the way Alex looked at her was gratifying.

"Boy, Alex, you'll do anything to get Kelly's attention!" Paisley teased.

Alex grinned, not taking his eyes off Kelly's face. "Just about anything," he admitted, and Kelly felt her heart flutter.

"There, what did I tell you," Paisley whispered as he moved away. "He's nuts about you, and considering all the gorgeous girls he works with day after day, that's quite a compliment."

"Look, Paisley," Kelly explained patiently, "I do like Alex, but for totally different reasons than yours." *Including making Eric jealous,* she thought. "There's a lot to Alex, you know. He has a mind of his own. And he's also a serious photographer. He doesn't want to make a career out of this kind of studio work. He'll be a famous artist someday."

"Oh, yeah? Has he asked you into the darkroom to see what develops?"

"Alex is a gentleman on a date," Kelly stated emphatically, ignoring the terrible joke. "Now will you leave me alone? I can only be serious about one boy at a time, and right now that boy is Eric Powers."

"You're impossible," Paisley cried in frustration. "And someday you'll really regret it if you let Alex slip through your fingers."

"Paisley," Kelly warned.

"Just friendly advice." Paisley crossed her fingers over her mouth. "Not another word, I promise."

"Okay, cut the chatter," Steve announced. "Paisley—tilt your chin much higher. And, Kelly—try to pretend you're having a good time."

Kelly laughed. *Click!* Lights flashed, a blinding light that Kelly never got used to. She marveled that her photos didn't show her cringing in anticipation of the flash.

"Alex," Steve ordered, "move that spot to the left—without injuring anyone, if you can."

Alex bristled but made a joke out of it. "I'll try not to start any fires, either."

Kelly had to admire the way Alex handled Steve, who could be nasty when he got into a bad mood. When that happened, everyone suffered.

Alex was so good at dealing with people, not in the least shy or awkward, as Eric sometimes was. Alex did have a lot of wonderful qualities, but something about the way Paisley tried to push Alex and her together only made Kelly resist stubbornly, furious that Paisley ignored Eric's role in Kelly's life completely.

"Hey," Steve called from his perch atop the ladder, "let's have some happy smiles down there!"

Kelly smiled so hard her face hurt.

"That's it," Steve called. "On to the next setup."

After taking shots of the models in sundresses and rompers, Steve finally called, "That's a wrap."

"Hooray." Paisley lowered her arms; she had been standing next to a "window," holding back curtains as "sunshine" from a spotlight reflected off a white backdrop and poured onto her flowered sundress. "Last one out of this place is *crazy*," she said, heading for the dressing room.

Kelly followed close behind, grateful the long assignment was at an end.

"Hey, Kelly." Alex stopped her. "How about some dinner? You don't have other plans, do you?"

"Don't keep the man waiting," Paisley said. "I wouldn't pass up that invitation."

"Then why don't you come to dinner, too," Alex said.

"I accept," Paisley declared, smiling in delight.

There was no reason not to go. Going out with Paisley and Alex would take her mind off Eric. Besides, Alex *was* fun company and would take them to a wonderful restaurant. And with Paisley along, there would be no danger that Alex might think Kelly was more interested in him than she was.

"I'd love a nice friendly dinner," Kelly said. "I'll be ready in a minute."

Inside the dressing room, Paisley sounded very smug. "You see—Alex made the first move, now go for it."

"I didn't say yes for the reasons you think," Kelly insisted. "So don't try to push the two of us together. I only want to have a nice dinner with someone who happens to think I'm special."

"Not like . . . oops." Paisley clapped a hand over her mouth. "Let's not mention that name."

Secretly, Kelly agreed. Right now, Eric was the last person she wanted to think about.

Five

"So now I've eaten at the famous Ernie's." Paisley twisted to take another look for celebrities. "Not a very fancy place—but it draws *quite* a crowd."

"It's enormous," Kelly said, raising her voice to be heard over the din. "And . . . popular."

"Noisy, you mean." Alex smiled. "I guess movie stars like a lot of excitement around. My dad takes me here sometimes. He signs a lot of deals over dinner, you'd be surprised."

"I'm surprised they can discuss deals in this noise."

At a distant table, someone spotted Alex and waved. Paisley grabbed his arm.

"Who's that—someone famous? Anyone I'd know?" She craned her neck to get a better look.

"Relax—a business associate of Dad's." Alex scanned the crowd. "There's no one I know here who's really famous. . . . Oh, there's Michelle Oliver."

Paisley frowned. "What's she been in?"

"She's not an actress," Alex explained. "She owns a photography gallery. But she does show photos by celebrities."

Paisley gasped. "I've heard of her." She held a hand over her heart. "Introduce us, Alex, please."

"Paisley, you don't need to meet a gallery owner," Kelly chided her. "But, Alex, you should show Michelle your work. Does she know you're a good photographer?"

"I'm not ready for a show at the Oliver Gallery," Alex said.

Paisley sprang into action. "Never look a gift horse in the mouth—you never know who *they* know!" Without another word, she was crossing the vast room, headed straight for Michelle Oliver's table.

"Oh, no," Kelly groaned. "This is too much."

Alex stood up. "I'd better stop her before she does something embarrassing."

"I'll go with you."

By the time they reached the other table, Paisley was deep in conversation with Michelle Oliver and her companions, particularly with a young man she introduced as "a promising actor."

"It's nice to see you again, Alex." Michelle Oliver shook his hand warmly. "How's your father?"

"He's well, thanks—and I'm sorry to have bothered you."

"Oh, but ask her about your photos," Paisley said.

"Really, Paisley," he protested, "I don't have much of a portfolio yet. . . ."

"When you do, I'd be glad to take a look at it," Michelle offered.

"Thanks." Alex grabbed Paisley's arm. "Oh—I think our food has come. Goodbye, Michelle."

Grimly, he marched Paisley back to their table.

"What's the matter with you?" she complained, rubbing her arm. "We already finished eating, and I was only trying to help."

Alex suppressed a smile. "Thanks, Paisley, but I'll help myself—when I'm ready."

"I'll bet you're ready now," Paisley said. "I know—why don't you let Kelly judge? She has a *fabulous* eye for photography."

"I do not," Kelly protested.

"Don't be so modest—you know you do. Kelly could say if you're ready for the Oliver Gallery."

"That would be great." Alex turned to Kelly. "You could come to my apartment—all my work is there."

"Maybe some other time," Kelly stalled.

"There's no time like the present," Paisley bubbled. "Unless you're *afraid* to go to his apartment."

"Of course I'm not. But . . . it's awfully late. I'd have to let my parents know. . . ."

"Good idea!" Paisley sprang up, gathering her things together. "Well, dinner was divine and it's been a lovely night, Alex, but I have to run."

Kelly stared. "Aren't you coming along?"

"*Goodness* no—I have another date." Paisley checked her watch. "In fact, I have two dates—and one is with that *gorgeous* young actor we just met. Of course, I'll have to get away somehow, to show up for my other date." She laughed lightly. "What a predicament this is! Oh, well, I'll think of something. See you guys!" She blew a kiss and left.

Kelly and Alex burst out laughing.

"I don't believe her," Kelly said. "She's incredible."

"She is. But I like her."

"Me, too."

Alex signaled for the waiter. "I'll pay the check while you make that phone call," he said.

Kelly's sister, Tina, answered on the second ring, clearly disappointed when she heard Kelly's voice.

"Tina—is Mom home?"

"They went to a movie."

"Leave a note that I'll be late, okay?"

"You're already late. Mom said you'd be home by the time I went to bed tonight."

"You don't need a sitter, Tina. You're thirteen—that's old enough to stay alone."

"Where are you? Mom will want to know."

"I'm having dinner with Alex," she said curtly.

"Oh, good!" Tina exclaimed. "Alex is much better than Eric."

"Thanks, Tina," Kelly said sarcastically. "Just tell Mom and Daddy—"

"Mom will be thrilled you're out with Alex. She wants you to marry him, I think."

"Tina," Kelly warned.

"When you're older, of course—maybe eighteen. He's rich, isn't he, and he's awfully cute, too. . . ."

"Just tell them I'll be late."

"Where are you and Alex going?"

Kelly hung up on her.

* * *

Alex threw a match into the fireplace, and the kindling caught and flared in a burst of flames. "I love a fire," Alex said. "I'm glad winter is coming."

"Me, too." Kelly couldn't help staring around the room. It seemed so luxurious for Alex to have such a large apartment all to himself. She only hoped her parents would allow her to live on campus instead of at home when she went to college. But to have an apartment all to herself, one that had a living room with a fireplace, a view of the trees in Washington Square Park, a deep red rug on the floor, and a sleek modern sofa and two leather armchairs—that was beyond hope.

Absently, she cradled in both hands the brandy glass Alex had given her.

"How is that? Not too strong for you . . ."

"It's fine," Kelly lied, taking a tiny sip. She'd wanted coffee, but when Alex suggested the brandy, she'd agreed, afraid to seem unsophisticated. Paisley had made her so self-conscious!

"That's right—warm the glass with your hands," Alex told her. "It brings out the flavor."

"Oh, I knew that," she said, although she really hadn't.

Actually, the room was a little small and close for a fire since the fall night wasn't very chilly. To avoid the heat, Kelly wandered to the brick wall opposite the fireplace. She was startled to find herself eye to eye with a framed photograph of a nude woman sprawled on her back in strong sunlight.

"Is this one of yours?" She swirled her brandy, trying to appear nonchalant, as if she were perfectly used to drinking in a man's apartment, alone with him and a photograph of a nude.

"I wish," Alex said reverently. "That's an Edward Weston. One of the foremost photographers of our time."

"It must be valuable." Instinctively, Kelly backed away from it.

"Somewhat." Alex took her glass away. "You don't like your drink—I'll get you something else."

"Actually, I'd like to see your photographs," she said, hoping Alex hadn't done any nude studies. She sat down on the sofa.

"Are you really interested?" Before she could answer, he was digging through a closet for a large black leather portfolio, which he spread across the coffee table before sitting next to Kelly. "These are my latest. I like the laundromat series best."

Kelly stared at abstract patterns and black and white compositions. "These are a laundromat?"

"You don't like them."

"No, no, I think they're very good. I just wouldn't have recognized what they were."

"That's the idea," Alex said eagerly. "You're not supposed to recognize them—they're supposed to present something familiar in a totally unfamiliar way."

Kelly eyed the photos with a new understanding. "I see—you concentrated on the shapes and colors and patterns of things we take for granted."

"Exactly." Alex turned over more photos in the series.

"I like them," Kelly said.

"Really?"

"They're original, and they're very well done."

She held a photo up to catch the light. "Did you do your own printing and everything?"

"Everything—from start to finish. That's one thing you can't do in commercial work, like at Steve's studio, where you have to send things out for developing and printing. Someday, I'd like to do nothing but my own work."

"I hope you get to do it," Kelly remarked. "I admire artists."

Alex took the photographs from her hand. "I admire you . . . for admiring artists."

He leaned over and kissed her. "Ummm . . . nice," he said. He touched her hair, then ran a finger gently along the side of her face. Playfully, he tapped her nose, then softly traced the outline of her lips.

"Alex . . . maybe we shouldn't do this."

"Why not?" He kissed her lightly. "It's nice, isn't it? I know you think so." He kissed her again and her eyes closed automatically. He smelled of lemony after-shave.

"Wait a minute." Kelly pulled away.

"What's wrong?" Alex frowned. "We're not doing anything we haven't done already."

"That's not true. Kissing you after a date is . . . is different from kissing you here." She felt stupid saying it out loud, but that's exactly what she was thinking. "Kissing you here"—she struggled not to sound ridiculous—"well, it's more serious or something. Maybe we shouldn't start."

"But we already have." He looked at her quizzically, then leaned over to kiss her again.

"No, don't. Look, Alex, I'm sorry if this is crazy," she said. "I know I've kissed you before. I know this time isn't any different just because we're here, but . . ."

"But what? What's going on? . . . Are you afraid?" His gray eyes showed concern.

I think you're afraid, Paisley's mocking words echoed.

"Of course not," she said. "I've already kissed you. I'm not afraid of you."

"Good. Then there's no problem."

Alex leaned toward her again, and she sat back until she was pressing against the couch. The room was warm from the fire, and she was tired after the long session of work. Kelly let herself sink into the deep cushions. Alex was only holding her now, anyway. It was comfortable and cozy. Maybe it was all right.

Then, when she least expected it, he kissed her again. This time the kiss was longer and more insistent. She went limp all over, responding to his kiss—until his hand trailed lightly along her side and she flinched. Alex lifted his hand. He tried to kiss her again, but she turned her head away.

"Wait, it's—it's too warm in here," she stuttered. "Uh . . . the fire is bothering me. . . ."

"Is it? I can open the window. . . . How's that? Any better?"

The bamboo shade scraped against the windowsill in the breeze.

"Much better. Isn't it funny how the weather changes so fast at this time of year?" She laughed, a little nervously, and Alex looked at her strangely.

"Yeah, it's funny."

"Well, you really have a beautiful apartment, but it must be getting late and maybe I should get going—"

Alex grabbed her hand. "Don't run away. You *are* afraid of me, aren't you?"

She flushed. "Of course not. Only . . . only of our getting . . . carried away." She gritted her teeth, sure he would laugh out loud, but instead he turned off the light behind the couch and put his arms around her again.

"We won't get carried away," he promised. He kissed her mouth, then her cheek, and began to nuzzle her neck.

"Kelly . . . ," he murmured, "you feel so good. . . ."

"Alex, stop. . . . Come on, I have to go. . . ."

He sat up and laughed. "Boy, I knew you were different from other girls I've dated, but not *this* different." He twisted a lock of her hair around his finger. "We'll take it slow, I promise."

She pulled away. "Alex, I hate it when you tell me how cute and innocent I am. Maybe I have other reasons for acting the way I do."

"What other reasons?" Alex asked smugly.

"You're so incredibly sure of yourself. Maybe you don't know everything, Alex Hawkins. Maybe it just so happens I could be interested in someone else—ever think of that?"

"Oh . . ." The light went out of Alex's eyes, and for a moment she felt a surprising stab of regret. "Oh, so that's it. You're right, I didn't think of that, but obviously, I should have. Someone else, huh. Well, maybe you enjoyed stringing me along. I suppose I should congratulate you for being so clever."

"You're jealous," she said in shock.

"And you're glad," he retorted.

"No, Alex, it's not like that at all. This is terrible—I didn't do this on purpose."

Alex snapped on the light. "Don't you know better than to lead a guy on like that? Didn't you think it might be dangerous to come here with me if you weren't even interested in me?"

"Of course I'm interested in you. I like you a lot. But not that way. . . . I mean, I didn't come here like you say, on purpose."

"You mean you came here by mistake?"

"Don't tease me, I know it doesn't make sense." Kelly groaned. "Oh, Alex—sometimes I feel like such an idiot, but it's only . . . it's only that I'm so new at this! I've messed everything up."

"New at what?"

She took a deep breath. "Well, at . . . boys. Don't laugh, please. I . . . I never really had boyfriends before. Not real ones, not grown-up boyfriends. I guess . . . I don't know how to act."

Alex stared at her. "Are you serious? Kelly, I thought you were unsophisticated and not very experienced—but not *this* inexperienced! I can't believe it."

"Well, believe it," she said miserably. "The only boyfriend I ever had was Danny Marks, who liked me better than I liked him. He hounded me all through junior high, and if you want to know the truth, I was relieved when his family moved in ninth grade."

Alex laughed in disbelief. "Come on, there must have been other boys."

"No, and certainly never anyone like you."

"What do you mean, like me?"

"You know. . . . You flatter me all the time,

and you're always trying to impress me, and you're so sophisticated . . ."

"Other boys must have tried to impress you."

"They didn't. Honestly, you have no idea what I'm really like, Alex. Boys never liked me. I wasn't pretty that way. I never dreamed I'd become a model. I never thought I had the right kind of looks."

"You? If anyone looks like a model, you do."

"But I never thought so. I still think of myself as a scrawny little kid. Sometimes my hair's too kinky, and my mouth is too full—"

"Well, you're definitely not conceited," Alex said glumly. "Every other girl I know thinks she's beautiful enough to be a model, and isn't. You're the exact opposite—a heartbreaker, and you don't know it."

"Because no one ever made a fuss over me before," she said honestly. "Ask the boys at school—they're amazed I'm a model now! My own mother was always begging me to dress up or wear makeup. The only thing I paid attention to was my hair."

"I can see why." Alex lifted a heavy lock.

"Don't, Alex. I'm trying to explain something."

"Okay, I'll sit here with my hands folded and stay out of trouble."

Kelly took a deep breath. "I became a model almost by accident, because my friend Jennifer dragged me to the beauty make-over at the mall where Meg Dorian discovered me." Kelly laughed ruefully. "That's when I was more interested in track than in modeling. But you know, Alex, something happened—once I started modeling, once people told me I could be good, that I had what it takes—once I got the taste of being really good at something, I got hooked."

"You're good at track, aren't you?"

She shook her head. "Good, but I work hard at it. I'm not a natural. Modeling comes easy to me. It's something I'm good at, just by being me. I've never been the best before. And I have to admit, even though I still don't believe I'm beautiful, it's thrilling to have people tell me I am. And that's part of the reason I like being with you—you make me feel like I'm beautiful and adventurous and fun to be with. But I'm not used to being that way yet."

"You are those things. That's why I like you, Kelly. I like you a lot. And you liked me, too, right away. I could tell."

She thought of how they'd met: Steve Hollender was taking publicity shots for a gala charity ball at which Kelly was doing her first runway modeling. Alex had attended the ball the next night and had rescued her from a near disaster. That was the first time he'd kissed her, and she'd been startled but pleased. She *had* liked Alex, but not the same way she liked Eric.

"No, you're wrong," she insisted. "I mean, I like you—but not that way."

"I don't believe you. You came over here tonight—and you knew what would happen. You wanted me to kiss you, you wanted me to make the first moves."

"No, I didn't," she insisted, but her conscience pricked. "Well, maybe I did know you'd kiss me, but I didn't want to come. Don't you remember? I said it was too late, I said some other time would be better."

"Then why did you come?"

"Well, for one thing, because of Paisley—she

said I was afraid. I wanted to prove she was wrong."

Alex winced. "Thanks a lot."

"And, to be completely honest, I thought it would make this other boy, Eric, jealous. But I didn't mean to hurt your feelings. I guess I wasn't thinking very clearly. . . . This is so confusing. . . ."

"Jealousy is nothing to play at."

Alex had turned toward the fire, and in the golden light his face looked soft and vulnerable. She felt a rush of tenderness. She did like Alex and she wanted to comfort him, but since Alex wanted more than a friend, that would only make things worse.

"You're right, Alex—jealousy isn't anything to play at. For one thing, I made the wrong boy jealous, and I can see now that it causes more hurt than anything else. Making Eric jealous wouldn't have done me any good. And it was terribly unfair to you. I made a mistake. I'm sorry."

"Look," Alex said, "I really don't care if there is someone else. The Hawkins men are all fighters, and I think I should warn you—we can be very persuasive. You might find you want me after all. But let's be straight with each other, no playing one guy against the other, okay?"

"Okay. Thanks. I'm glad we're still friends. You were right about something else, Alex. I do like you a lot."

"Now you're flattering me. You're not making this easy."

What do *I want? Alex is everything a girl could want. Tina thinks he's a god, and Mom is thrilled whenever I mention him. Everyone loves Alex. Except me.*

"But, I'm willing to put up with you, inexperience and all," Alex said smugly. "I'll bet I win. And in the meantime, Kelly, we can do things any way you'd like. Should we kiss and make up?"

"Alex," she said warningly.

"Okay, okay—we'll just be friends." He picked up her hand and shook it.

"Maybe," she said with a sigh of relief, "maybe that's best for now."

Alex kissed her politely on the cheek. "To friendship," he said softly.

"Thanks, Alex. I'm glad you understand. Maybe if I'd met you first . . ."

"Don't tell me that. I don't need excuses. This is a fair fight. Just make sure you warn your pal Eric he's got heavy competition on his hands."

She laughed. "Everyone I know has some heavy competition to deal with." Alex's eyes were clear and sparkling now. *Why, he enjoys this!* she thought. *He enjoys having to fight for me!*

"Isn't it crazy how things work out," she murmured, staring into the fire. The more she wanted Eric, the more Alex seemed to want her.

Six

"Hi, stranger."

Eric looked up at her. He was doing leg pulls and stretches against the first plank of the bleachers. "Kelly, hi!" He flushed and straightened.

"Oh, don't stop," she said, "finish your warm-ups. I haven't seen you over here lately." What a dumb thing to say—as the best cross-country runner, Eric was always highly visible at practice.

Kelly was the one who had missed practices lately, because of her modeling jobs. She did work out on her own to make up for it, running through the neighborhood at night with her father following in the family car. And when she was able to attend practice, she tried to do twice as much twice as hard. Still, she always felt as if Coach Hayes were watching her, waiting for her to slip, and then he would ask her to leave the team.

"Haven't seen you around school much lately, either," Eric commented.

Kelly lowered her eyes. It was true—she hadn't seen much of Eric since the night they made dinner together at his house. But it wasn't because of her work, although she had been incredibly busy lately. She had purposely avoided Eric, hoping he would start to miss her if she wasn't around so much. It was part of her plan.

"Yeah, I've been really busy, and you know how it is," she said, grinning up at him. "You hate to turn down work—they might not ask you the next time."

"Ever the career girl," Eric quipped.

Coach Hayes, his whistle bouncing over his rather large belly, approached them.

"Stretch those hamstrings, Powers—you can give your mouth a workout some other time."

He stopped to wipe the sweat off his forehead. "Glad to see you made practice, Blake."

"I've been running every night," she said. "I'm in really good shape."

"Good—because I need you at the Franklyn-Edison meet. The flu has nearly wiped out the rest of the girls—got to have someone strong running."

"No problem," Kelly said. "I'm in great shape—we'll lick them easily."

Coach Hayes nodded mildly. "We'll put up a fight, anyway. Okay—get going now. There isn't much time left till Thursday."

"Thursday?" Kelly snapped to attention, staring in dismay. "Isn't the meet tomorrow?"

"Thursday at four-thirty. Home meet." Coach

Hayes pinned her with a searching look. "This after-school job of yours isn't going to interfere, is it?"

For some reason, the coach refused to use the right terms for Kelly's modeling work, preferring to describe it as her "after-school job"—perhaps to make her seem more like the other kids, because kids with after-school jobs were a familiar problem for Coach Hayes. Kelly was his first athlete who was also a model.

"There is a small problem," Kelly admitted. "I, uh—" She hesitated. One more excuse and cross-country would be finished for her. "Well, see, I won't be in school on Thursday. I'm . . ."—she mumbled the rest—"shooting my first television commercial."

"Television?" Coach Hayes spat on the ground, clearly unimpressed by her big news. "What do I care about television?"

"Be fair, Coach," Eric said. "This is a big break for Kelly. She can't do everything."

"Listen, Coach," Kelly said, glancing at Eric, "the shoot can't take all day. I'll be at the studio at ten-thirty A.M., and I can't imagine working more than five hours. I just have three sentences to say."

Coach Hayes eyed her narrowly. "Then I can count on you?"

"Absolutely. I wouldn't let you down."

"You won't get another chance to let me down," he said sourly. "Season's almost over."

"I know I owe it to you," she said, "but this can be my chance to make up for all the times I've missed. You can count on me."

The coach clapped her on the back. "That's the

stuff," he said approvingly. "Now you two take off—we're losing light."

"Thanks," she called as the coach moved away.

"You really meant that, about making it up to Coach, didn't you?" Eric said.

"I'm trying to be a responsible person."

"I admire that. I really do."

She smiled in pleasure. "How about a two-mile run?"

"Not with me," he said. "You can't match my speed."

"Try me," she challenged.

Eric wrapped his sweatshirt around his neck. "We'll keep it to a slow run." But he took off at top speed.

"Hey!" Startled, Kelly stood there for a minute, then had to really sprint to catch up.

Eric grinned as she came up alongside him. "You're not bad, Blake. Anyway, it's great you still care about the team, although you must be pretty excited about shooting the commercial."

"I am," Kelly admitted. "And guess what? Julie Higgins asked me to speak to the Drama Club about it. They want to know all about acting for television."

"Julie Higgins? She's not a friend of yours, is she?"

"Oh, we've always spoken, although we're not close or anything. But she seems pretty nice once you get to know her. Kids can be prejudiced against the popular crowd, too, just because they think they aren't wanted. I mean, I used to snub Julie and Patty Berg because I thought they were snubbing me. So I was a snob, too."

"That's funny," Eric said mildly. "Julie and Patty have always been nice to me. They always ask me to their parties."

"I heard they did, but then, they're cheerleaders, they're so involved with sports . . ." Kelly's words trailed off vaguely. She'd been on the track team, involved with sports all year, and she'd never been asked to their parties before.

"I never enjoyed their parties too much," Eric said. "But maybe now . . . if you go to them, too—"

"I'd love that!" Just in time, she remembered to keep things light, not to put any pressure on Eric. "It would be fun if more of my friends got into their crowd, wouldn't it? We'd have a ball, and it would be good for school spirit, too."

"Is that all you think about, the school?" He smiled teasingly.

"No, of course not. I just thought it might be a lot of fun if we all went."

"You'll probably be so busy acting now you won't go, anyway."

"Don't worry about that. My part in the commercial isn't all that impressive. 'Balmour's has casuals for everybody's baby,'" she said mockingly. "Some acting debut!"

"You have to start somewhere."

"Jennifer says it should be, 'Balmour's has contempt for anybody's baby,'" she panted, "because they're so overpriced."

"I think she's right. How about, 'Balmour's bleeds the best.'"

"'Balmour's means bankruptcy.'"

"'Balmour's breaks bank accounts. . . .'"

Laughing, they stumbled past the end of the football field. By the time they were running smoothly again, they were at the far end, where the path joined the edge of the woods that separated the school property from the parkway.

Fallen leaves were everywhere, crunching underfoot.

When Kelly was little, she and her friends used to pack sandwiches and ride their bikes along the paved sidewalks running beside the parkway. They would stop and picnic in a grassy place overhung with huge trees, and pretend they were someplace in the country.

"When I was a kid," Kelly said, "we used to bring picnics down here in summer and pretend it was a big country meadow. It was so pretty then."

"It's pretty now," Eric said. "Fall is my favorite season. Pretty, but sad too—all the leaves dying. Like a beginning and an ending, all together."

She stared at him and he blushed at his spontaneous poetry.

"I guess that sounded dumb."

"No, I agree with you, only I couldn't have said it so beautifully. You put it just right."

Eric took the turn into the wooded section, running between the tall trees.

"You're in pretty good shape," he said.

"Thanks." But she was feeling a definite strain, keeping up with Eric's stride.

"It must be tough, running and working, too."

"My dad helps—couldn't do it alone. I run nights if I have a job that day. . . . He follows, in the car—oh, I have to stop."

Eric looked around awkwardly as Kelly broke off the trail. She leaned against a tree.

"Stitch in my side," she gasped.

Uncertainly, he ran back to where she was leaning.

"You go ahead," she managed to say. *Darn—*

here I am trying to impress him, and instead I crumple like a rag doll. The pain in her side throbbed.

"You should run through it." She could see by Eric's expression that he was afraid she'd resent his advice. His hair, tousled from the running, flopped over one eye. He looked strong, and concerned—and adorable.

It's no use! I can't pretend to be so cool; I just can't keep up this game. Suddenly she felt like crying. She turned her head aside so Eric couldn't see the longing expression in her eyes.

"You've been avoiding me, haven't you?" Eric's voice was grave.

"I've just been busy," she said. "You're the one who hasn't been around."

"Twice this week, I waited by your locker in the morning. You never showed."

"I didn't know," she insisted.

"I should have called you, I guess."

"You didn't have to."

He shrugged.

"So," she said with pretended indifference, "how was the weekend . . . with what's-her-name?" He turned pale and she could have bitten her tongue. "Forget I said that—I don't care." She should have kept her big mouth shut. She was giving herself away, acting too interested in Rissa. Next time, she'd wait for Eric to mention the other girl.

Eric broke a leaf off a tree and crumpled it aimlessly. Suddenly they heard other runners approaching.

"You'd better go," Kelly said.

But instead of leaving, Eric grabbed her by the arm. "Come on—we need to talk." He pulled her deeper into the woods, away from the path. "How's your side now?"

"Better."

"I didn't say anything about the weekend because I thought it would upset you," he explained. "Really—it was nothing."

"I'm sure." *Careful, Kelly. Find out but don't show your true feelings*. "I guess her parents like you a lot."

He shrugged. "I guess so."

"So if they like you," she hinted, "they wouldn't mind leaving you alone with—what's-her-name, right?"

Eric colored, and Kelly immediately imagined the worst—Eric and Rissa, taking a romantic stroll at night, arm in arm, stopping to kiss under a street light . . .

"What did you do this weekend?" Eric retorted. "I suppose you and your hot-rodder pal made the scene, with all his rich, hotshot city friends . . ."

"As a matter of fact," she explained, "I had a very dull weekend. I worked on Friday. Then I was supposed to sleep over at Jennifer's on Saturday night, but I guess she had too much studying, so she canceled it. She's been acting funny lately. I guess she's worried about that computer course."

"You mean you stayed home? I . . ." He hesitated. "I assumed you were with . . . with what's-his-name . . ."

Kelly held back a pleased smile—so Eric couldn't say Alex's name out loud, just as she couldn't bear to say Rissa's. Things were looking up.

"I haven't seen Alex for days."

"Doesn't he call you?"

"It's not that kind of thing. We're just friends, you know—I don't have to see him. Besides, he's very busy, with classes full time and his job."

"The big college man," Eric muttered.

"You'd like Alex," Kelly said. "You have a lot in common—"

"Yeah, I'm a rich college man, too," Eric said sarcastically.

"Not that—but you both work hard, and—"

"And we've both kissed you."

"Eric!" She colored; then, to her surprise and dismay, she felt tears form in her eyes. She wanted him to be jealous, but not to give up. If he thought she was seriously interested in Alex, Eric would never pursue her—he was too honorable. This could really backfire!

He stared at her, shocked. "Don't cry. . . ."

"It's nothing—allergies . . ." How could she explain it to him? "It has nothing—to do with you," she gulped, breaking down completely.

"Kelly . . . Hey, come on, please . . ." He put his arms around her, soothing her as if she were a child. "Please don't cry."

"It's—" She pushed him away. Thank goodness there was a crumpled tissue in the pocket of her sweat jacket. "It's—the strain, I guess," she improvised. "Working, and"—she inhaled, making a raspy sound—"and pressure—school, and Coach—" She wiped her eyes.

"I'm sorry—I didn't know you had it so rough."

"Don't feel sorry for me."

"I tried to explain about Rissa," Eric said gently. "If that's bothering you. She's just not good at being alone."

"Alone!" Kelly sniffed. "You said she's so popular—when is she alone?"

"You know what I mean—alone, like without a boyfriend . . ."

"You moved here months ago," Kelly said skeptically. "What makes you think she's still so alone? Do you really believe she's never dated anyone else—not even casually?"

Eric looked uncomfortable. "Well, casually . . ." he said vaguely.

"Yeah—and probably doesn't tell you anything about it. I know the type—she has to have every boy in love with her. You don't know what really goes on, Eric. She's probably just stringing you along."

There must have been some truth to what Kelly was saying. Eric looked away. "I guess I don't know what goes on," he admitted softly. He looked so hurt that Kelly immediately regretted her remarks.

"I'm sorry—" Helplessly, Kelly reached for him. "I only said that because I was angry. I'll bet she's been true to you." Suddenly Kelly laughed out loud. "Am I crazy—convincing you your ex-girl is true to you! The female population of Franklyn, New Jersey, will kill me!"

Eric laughed, too, and they turned to each other and embraced. "I hate to see you cry," he said.

"It was silly. . . ."

"You were right to say what you did." Eric frowned. "People shouldn't hold on to each other for the wrong reasons. Maybe I should call it off between Rissa and me."

Kelly's spirits leaped. *Stay calm, don't show*

anything or you'll scare him away. "Well, do what you think is best," she said vaguely.

"Maybe it doesn't make sense. But Rissa says she needs me and she isn't like most girls. . . . She's not as strong as you."

"I'm not so strong," Kelly said quickly. "And she's probably not that weak—but I think you're right not to get more involved," she added.

"Hey, Powers," someone called through the trees. "Is that you?"

Three guys from track were passing. "Bringing up the rear?" one taunted. "Or joining the girls' team?"

"Betcha can't catch me," Tommy Fuller hooted.

"Who can't—" Without a backward glance, Eric turned and sprinted toward the other boys, leaving Kelly alone with the trees and the fallen leaves.

Rissa can't be as helpless as she pretends to be. I'll bet she's really stringing Eric along. He'll find out when he gets fed up with Rissa's clinging—especially when he sees how much fun it can be with me around.

Footsteps pounded and the rest of the girls' cross-country team appeared at the head of the path—not that Kelly cared if anyone had seen her alone in the woods with Eric. Nevertheless, she hurried to the edge of the clearing and knelt, as if tightening her shoelaces. Seconds later, Amanda Collins and Sue Levine came crashing through the trees, ahead of the pack.

"Kelly," Sue called, "what happened?"

"These dumb shoes," Kelly muttered vaguely, joining them. "Ruined my time . . ."

"Looked to me like you were making good time," Sue said with a conspiratorial wink.

Kelly glanced at Sue, who was captain of the girls' track team. She had a steady boyfriend, a freshman at a college in Connecticut. *How do they manage a long-distance romance*, Kelly wondered. She had an impulse to tell Sue about Eric and Rissa and ask her advice, but Amanda would hear everything.

"Maybe I'll get a new pair of shoes," Kelly said slyly. "These shoes might be too much trouble." Her eyes followed Eric, running ahead.

"Sometimes they're worth the trouble, sometimes they're not," Sue said wisely. "But a girl only needs one really good pair of shoes."

Kelly grinned at Sue's clever way of putting things.

"Who cares about shoes?" Amanda grumbled.

Kelly and Sue burst out laughing, ignoring Amanda's baffled look.

"What's so funny?" she demanded.

"Amanda, just keep running."

Kelly grinned at Sue, enjoying their private joke. The boys widened the distance between them, sprinting toward the two-mile mark. *Running is a lot like romance*, Kelly thought—*there may be a lot of competition in the pack when you start, but at the finish line, there's only one winner—the person who cared the most, the one who stayed the distance.*

Seven

"I'm really glad you could come with me to the city today, Jen." Kelly fussed in her model's bag, making sure she'd brought everything she might need for the commercial shoot.

"I'm glad you still wanted me to."

"Well, of course I did. I'm a little nervous about this. I'm just glad your mom let you miss school today."

"My mom was as excited as I am about seeing a real commercial made," Jennifer said. "We're lucky she didn't come along!"

"If she had, she could have helped take notes, too. I don't want you to miss one detail. I have to remember everything for my talk to the Drama Club."

"Don't worry," Jennifer said, "I'm sure Julie and Patty will be suitably impressed."

"Good," Kelly said, "because that's important to me."

"The Drama Club is important to you? What about the commercial you're about to shoot?"

"That's important, too." She giggled nervously. "Oh, Jen, I really *am* nervous. And I really am glad you came with me."

"I can afford to miss one day of school," Jennifer said. "Though I admit I was surprised my mom said yes. She's like that—sometimes she gets into the spirit of things and really surprises me. Like that time in ninth grade—remember?"

Jennifer glanced out the bus window as a New York taxi passed them, then turned back to Kelly. "I'll bet you'd forgotten that—our big shopping spree, the day I slept over your house! Boy, we used to have fun together."

"I remember that, we were supposed to study for an American civilization test. And we stayed up all night and never got any studying done, and the next morning we decided we couldn't face school, and why not go shopping instead? It was the first—and only—time I ever cut school."

"Me, too," Jennifer agreed. "It seemed like a lot of fun—the good girls acting bad for once. Until I got back home that afternoon, and realized I was carrying all those shopping bags, and how would I explain that to my mother when I was supposed to have been in school all day?"

"My folks were furious." Kelly remembered her father's outraged lecture about responsibility.

"I stashed the shopping bags in the bushes out front and tried to pretend nothing was wrong. I'll never forget the way my knees collapsed when my mother told me the school called to ask why I was absent. I thought she'd *kill* me."

"But she didn't."

"Nope. I thought she would've flipped out and panicked and called the police. Not my mom—'Oh, Jennifer has a sore throat today,' she told them!" Both girls laughed, remembering.

Jennifer beamed. "She even asked to see what I bought! Parents really surprise you sometimes."

"She knows you're a good kid," Kelly said. "I guess she figures you're allowed to cut loose once in a while."

"It's true. She said I'd be abnormal if I didn't." Jennifer sighed. "Sometimes I think I should be wild more often. I get tired of being good old reliable Jennifer, the one everyone can depend on. Maybe I should create a different image for myself. Maybe I'm being left behind."

"Don't be silly. I need you the way you are. And that's half the reason you're here with me today, because you *are* reliable and you'll be sure to get me back in time for the cross-country meet today."

Jennifer frowned. "Oh, that—I still think you should've pulled out of the meet. You may not make it in time."

"It might be close," Kelly agreed, "but if I miss this meet, I'm off the team for sure."

"What's the big deal? You barely have time for school and modeling and running. Why not make it easy on yourself and just quit—the season's nearly over, anyway."

"I can't quit," Kelly said simply. "Once I start something I don't give it up. I might fail or make a fool of myself, but I've never quit anything I got myself into. That's just the way I am."

"There's nothing wrong with that, I guess." The bus pulled into the Port Authority Bus

Terminal, and the girls made their way outside to the cab stand. They got inside the first cab in line, and Kelly gave the driver an address on East Ninety-fourth Street.

"Of course," Kelly added, "Eric will be at the meet today—and I want him to know I'm dedicated to track. But it's also a personal point of honor—I committed to it, and I want to do well. Just like I want to do well on all my modeling assignments."

"And, of course, Alex is at most of your modeling jobs. It must be tough, having two boyfriends to impress."

"Well, I'd give up Alex," Kelly insisted, "but he won't give *me* up. He's called me every night this week, asking for a date, because 'good friends' should see each other often!"

"I guess there's no reason *not* to see Alex," Jennifer said.

"It's hard to turn him down. You know how I feel about Eric, but it's exciting to be with Alex. He knows all kinds of people; he takes me to terrific places. You should have seen his eyes that night I got dressed up and we went dancing in the city! It would be hard to give him up. And just think, Jen, now that I'm an actress, I'll get to go to more of those places, and people may recognize me. Famous people that even Alex doesn't know! I'll be a real celebrity."

"Too good for us common folk."

"Don't be silly. I hate when you say things like that. Of course you'll see me."

The cab took a right-hand turn onto Ninety-fourth Street and slowed down. "Here we are," Jennifer said.

"My stomach is wall-to-wall butterflies." Kelly

stepped out of the cab behind Jennifer. "Jen, tell me I'll get through this all right. Tell me I have some acting talent and I can do this commercial!"

Jennifer sighed. "Don't worry. They gave you the job, didn't they? You'll do fine."

Taking a deep breath, Kelly opened the door and found herself in what looked like a run-down storage room, filled with huge cartons and tools and piles of unidentifiable junk.

"I'm Kelly Blake," she told a man in a glass-enclosed office. "For the Balmour's shoot."

"In the main soundstage," he told them. "Through those doors."

Kelly gasped when she and Jennifer had stepped through the double doors. This was more what she'd expected. They were in a huge space—a giant open room, full of lighting equipment and strewn with cables. Three sets took up most of the floor space—a kitchen, part of a gym, and a girl's bedroom, faithfully reproduced down to the last detail. Except for the fact that the walls were propped up from behind and there were no ceilings, the sections of rooms looked completely real.

The gym had a gleaming wooden floor and was equipped with real gymnastic apparatus and exercise mats. In one wall, a window was covered with chicken wire, and the walls and moldings looked as if they'd been repainted several times. There was even faded graffiti in one corner! It was an exact replica of a high-school gym.

A few feet away was the girl's bedroom. It, too, had a polished wooden floor, partially covered by a furry throw rug. The bed and windows sported matching fabric; a quilted flowered bedspread and fabric shades that looked as if they had just been pulled up to let in the morning sun. Makeup and jewelry cluttered the bureau—as if someone actually lived in the room and had just finished dressing. A framed photograph of a teenage boy stood on the night table next to the bed. Pictures and rock posters covered the walls.

"It's bizarre," Jennifer said. "How do they get those rooms in here?"

"They build them."

Kelly turned, and recognized the speaker, a woman named Mona who had been at her audition at the Three Doves Production Company.

"The set decorator designs it, the carpenter builds it, the painters put up the wallpaper, the propman adds the extra touches, and voilà! Real life." Mona grinned and shook Kelly's hand. "Good girl—you're right on time," she said. "And who's this?"

"My friend, Jennifer Lee." Kelly took a deep breath. "Mona, it's especially important that I leave promptly on time today."

"Sure you will," Mona said. "Now come with me. The stylist has some wardrobe for you." She raised her voice. "Patsy!"

Kelly wondered which of the hordes of people swarming around the set was the wardrobe stylist. She could eliminate those she recognized from her audition—Anita, the representative from Balmour's Department Stores; Ray, the man from the advertising agency; and Randy, the director, who was huddled in a corner with some of the technical staff.

"I didn't know there'd be so many people here," Kelly said uneasily, catching sight of the cameras. She felt a stab of pure fear. She had performed her audition in front of a video camera. But that had been tiny compared to the monstrous things—at least seven feet tall, with gigantic lenses—that were set up on the sound-stage. *How can I act naturally with those things pointed at me and so many people watching?*

A very tall, angular woman clutching an armful of clothing hurried toward them.

"Hi, I'm Patsy, your stylist. And you are . . . " She wavered, turning from Kelly to Jennifer.

"This one," Mona said, pushing Kelly forward.

Patsy sighed in relief. "Thank goodness! I thought someone gave me the wrong sizes. That's okay then," she said, measuring Kelly with her eye. "These should fit fine."

"Oh, this is my friend, Jennifer Lee," Kelly said hastily. "I asked her along to take notes on everything, for a presentation at our school. Everyone wants to know about acting for television."

"I don't blame them. It *sounds* like such a glamorous field," Patsy said. "But we'll cure you of that delusion today!" She winked. "Are you thinking of going into commercial production, Jennifer?"

"Oh, I don't have any acting talent."

"You don't have to. You could be a producer, like Mona, or a stylist, like me."

"What exactly is a stylist?" Jennifer asked, taking out her notebook and pen.

"The stylist coordinates all the clothes used in the commercial. Usually, I buy the wardrobe, working from a list of the actors' measurements. Clothes set the tone for the entire commercial. Today, of course, we'll use Balmour's fashions."

"You mean that's your *job?*" Jennifer exclaimed

incredulously. "You buy clothes for actors in commercials?"

"And return the ones that we don't use," Patsy added wistfully. "Hey, Jennifer, if you're not busy, I pay seventy-five dollars for someone to do returns for me. You just take the unused stuff back to the stores. It's all been charged to my account, so there's no problem."

"Seventy-five dollars? To take clothes back to a store?"

"Doesn't it sound like fun? What's your phone number?" Patsy began digging in her voluminous pockets for a pencil and paper. "I can really use extra help."

"I don't know." Jennifer frowned. "Isn't there a more creative job that I could do?"

"Jennifer, you're not looking for any job," Kelly reminded her. "Just take notes, okay?"

"She'll have to think about it," Mona said firmly. "Come on, girls, we have work to do. Grab some coffee and a piece of pastry if you're hungry, but, please—let's get a move on!"

"Always the clock-watcher," Patsy complained. "Jennifer, don't you go away. I could use a sensible kid like you."

"Oh, I'll be here all day," Jennifer answered. "We can talk more about those returns, if you'd like."

"Super!" Patsy beamed, filling a plate with doughnuts. "Maybe you could help me with Kelly's clothes."

"I'd love to," Jennifer said quickly. "Wow, look at all this food!"

"Shoots can get long and boring and tiring," Patsy explained. "You need something to keep people happy. Go ahead, Kelly, take something. I know it's not great for you, but you'll need all the extra energy you can get."

Kelly chose an herb tea and a plain croissant. "Listen, Jen," she whispered when Patsy and Mona were out of earshot, "don't try to butter people up like that. It's embarrassing."

"I'm not buttering anyone up. Patsy's nice, and I never heard of jobs like these before."

"You're a scientist, not a stylist. Besides, I need you to take notes for me."

"Believe it or not, I can take notes and talk at the same time," Jennifer shot back. "Don't worry about your big presentation, which is only a talk to the Drama Club, I might remind you. It's not the Academy Awards."

"But I'm counting on you for so many things today—taking notes, and getting me to the meet . . ."

"Oh, big intellectual challenges," Jennifer said sarcastically. "I really need to concentrate to do those things."

"Well, you're supposed to be helping me."

"Kelly, you haven't even started the commercial and you already have a star complex."

"I do not."

"You do, too. You're treating me like a servant. I'm not your slave."

"Come on, I never said you were. I just need you to help me today."

"Hey, you two—into the dressing rooms," Patsy commanded.

They followed her to a medium-sized bathroom at the front of the studio. "This is it?" Kelly had expected something larger, more like the dressing rooms she was used to in photographer's studios.

"I think it's wonderful," Jennifer said. "What did you expect? A Hollywood trailer with a star on the door?"

"No, I'm just used to something bigger," Kelly explained.

"I'm not," Jennifer said good-naturedly. "This is fantastic—look at those lights around the makeup mirror. Just like Hollywood!"

Patsy laughed delightedly. "I love real kids," she said.

"What do you usually work with? Imitation kids?" Jennifer joked.

Patsy burst into raucous laughter. "You're a doll," she said, slapping Jennifer's shoulder. "I like your friend," she told Kelly. "I'm glad you brought her along today."

"Me, too," Kelly said politely, although she was beginning to wish she hadn't.

"Well—to work. Here, try this blue outfit first," Patsy suggested, handing Kelly an impossibly sweet skirt-and-blouse combination, something she would never wear.

"Yech," Kelly said, not disguising her dislike of the ruffles and ribbons. "I don't have to wear that, do I?"

"I know," Patsy sighed. "Not my cup of tea, either—but you'll look super in it. Go on."

The clothes slipped on easily enough, but Kelly couldn't help making a face at the outfit in the mirror. "To think I'm going to be on television wearing *this*."

"Who cares what you're wearing," Jennifer said. "You'll be the Balmour's Girl—and the next time, you'll wear something better, I'll bet."

"There, that's the right attitude," Patsy approved. "A healthy smile and the right frame of mind is all you need. Remember, Kelly, they're paying you to make these clothes look good. So even if it's not what you'd choose yourself, you have to make other girls want to buy them."

"I guess I could try," Kelly said. "I mean, I am a professional. But this is sort of a letdown."

"Cheer up. Listen to your friend—Jennifer has the right attitude," Patsy told her.

Jennifer blushed modestly. At that moment, Kelly almost told Jennifer what she could do with her attitude.

"Ray! Anita!" Patsy yelled, pulling Kelly into the studio. "What do you think?"

Anita smiled widely. "That's wonderful—one of our most popular numbers. Very pretty."

"No, I don't think so." The advertising man scowled. "It's dull. Let's try something perkier, more spirited. The Balmour's Girl has spunk, individuality."

"I always liked that blue outfit," Anita protested.

"The orange," Ray said firmly.

Patsy nodded. "We'll try the orange."

As far as Kelly was concerned, the orange was equally bad. "I look awful in orange," Kelly sighed in front of the mirror.

"You look good in anything," Patsy said cheerily. "Keep a good frame of mind."

"It's wrong for the spot," Ray said this time. "I'll know the right look when I see it, when I see the outfit that says what we're trying to say to today's teen."

"Trying to say?" Kelly kidded Patsy, back in the dressing room. "I never heard clothes talk."

Patsy frowned. "Kelly," she said sternly, "you are *not* . . ."

". . . showing the right attitude," Kelly finished for her.

Patsy gave her a warning look, and Kelly knew she'd better watch her step.

"I'm sorry. It's just irritating, changing from outfit to outfit. Can't we get to the acting? That's what's important today."

Patsy smiled. "We'll get there. How about more coffee. Jennifer, would you mind?"

"Oh, not at all."

"Your friend is *terrific*," Patsy said.

They got lucky on the third outfit—a romantic dress in white linen, accessorized with a lace scarf and pearls.

"That's it," Anita declared, and for once everyone else agreed.

Kelly held out the full skirt of the dress. "I feel like I'm on my way to a square dance, but I love the lace."

Anita beamed. "That's one of our most popular looks. So many young girls long to be more romantic today."

"Oh, I know," Jennifer said dreamily, putting down full coffee cups. "Sometimes I think that if I dressed in fluffy outfits like these, the perfect boy would come and sweep me off my feet."

Kelly stared at her. "You *never* wear clothes like this. You're the tailored type."

"I know, that's what I mean—sometimes I wish I could be *different* from myself. Someone else, a romantic heroine!"

"Yes," Anita cried, "that's exactly the reaction we're looking for."

"Well, I'll try to remember that in my acting," Kelly said. *Romantic heroine, indeed,* she thought.

"Now let's get your hair and makeup done, and we'll be ready to roll," Mona announced.

Eight

"This set looks exactly like a real kitchen," Jennifer declared as they finally returned to the soundstage. "And look at the sunshine!"

"Those are spotlights," Kelly said, "set up outside the windows, to look like sunshine coming through."

"That's so clever!" Jennifer exclaimed, taking rapid notes. "This will be great stuff for your talk."

"My talk is supposed to be about acting. That's what people are interested in."

"Oh." Jennifer's pen wavered. "But the set design is wonderful. It looks exactly like someone's kitchen. Look at that dish towel draped over the oven door, the bowl of fruit on the table, and the magazines on the counter. And someone left tomatoes ripening on the windowsill! I never realized anyone designed all this stuff. I never even thought about it." Jennifer peered behind the kitchen walls, which were nothing but false fronts held up by wooden struts.

"I don't see why anyone would care about that. Wait for the acting, Jen. That's much more important."

"Okay, but I can't wait to describe these sets to someone. I hope there are lots of kids at the Edison meet."

"The meet!" Kelly glanced at the wall clock. It was almost noon—she had about three hours left if she wanted to get to the meet on time. "I hope we make it," she said.

"It couldn't possibly take more than three hours," Jennifer answered. "You only have a few lines!"

"You're right. It can't take long at all."

"Clear the set, please," Randy ordered.

Jennifer backed away to a safe place behind the cameras and the sound equipment while Kelly wiped her clammy palms off on her Balmour's skirt, hoping no one would notice. Mona came up to her.

"Exciting, huh?" She gave Kelly a squeeze.

"Who is that girl?" Kelly asked Mona, staring uneasily at a young woman posing for the camera in the kitchen set. Perhaps there'd been a mistake—or maybe Kelly didn't have the part. Maybe they'd replaced her because she'd complained about the clothes and taken so long in makeup. . . .

"That's Meredith," Mona quickly assured her. "She works for us. She's doing the lighting rehearsal—they take skin-tone readings from her, so that when you walk on the set, the camera will be ready to go. Saves time—and time is money."

Kelly breathed a silent sigh of relief. "Oh, I thought it was something like that," she said falsely. "But what are they doing now?"

"That's the soundman." Balancing a boom mike on a long pole, the soundman aimed the microphone toward Meredith while she spoke Kelly's lines. "He's adjusting the recording levels from her voice," Mona explained. "And the second assistant director and a production assistant are marking off the spots on the floor where you'll have to stand to be in focus for the camera."

"It seems as if the crew does everything," Kelly said.

"Everything except the acting—that job is all yours," Mona said.

Nervously, Kelly cleared her throat. "Balmour's has casuals . . . ," she muttered. *How loudly should I say my lines?* she wondered. She'd spent so many hours practicing in front of her mirror that now she panicked—what if she forgot everything!

Randy, the director, came over, and Mona, as if guessing how nervous Kelly was, patted her arm reassuringly as he approached.

"Doesn't Kelly look wonderful," Mona said. "And so relaxed—if she's this calm now, she'll be a wonderful actress." Mona winked at Kelly. "Have fun with it," she whispered.

Randy nodded. "Mona is right—the key is to be natural. Remember, you're an average, typical teenage girl. Up with fashion but not too sophisticated—you're thrilled when your boyfriend visits while you're baby-sitting. Got it? Tell me your lines."

"Balmour's has casuals for everybody's baby . . ."

"Good, fine—now we'll walk you through the piece," Randy said, signaling his assistant, Tony.

While Randy took his place behind the huge tripod that held the camera, Tony guided Kelly through the set.

"It really does look authentic," Kelly said, trying to act like a natural and typical teenage girl, "as if you could reach into the refrigerator and get a Coke."

"As a matter of fact," Tony said, "you have to do just that—only you pull out a baby bottle. Here's the routine."

He marched Kelly through the choreography, as he called it. "Action starts—you're with the baby at the high chair." He walked her to the kitchen table. "Baby eats food, you get up, cross here, *behind* the table, to the fridge—reach in, take out a baby bottle, shut the door, turn, walk back to the high chair, *behind* the table—cut! Next setup. There's a knock at the door, you look up, see your boyfriend, wave—cut!"

"Will he be here? The guy who plays my boyfriend?" Kelly hadn't seen any teenage boys on the set all morning.

"Separate shot," Tony said impatiently. "He's booked for late afternoon. You just worry about *your* part."

"You mean I pretend to react to him, but he isn't here."

"That's why we call it acting."

She hesitated; Tony had such a condescending manner. "Tony, I don't mean to bother you, but, uh, I want to get everything right," she said as sweetly as Jennifer would have. "Uh—don't I have to show off the clothes—I mean, don't you want me to twirl around or anything? In runway work, movement is the most important thing, and I really know how to show off an outfit's lines."

"Just worry about the choreography," Tony said archly. "We'll shoot close-ups of the clothes separately."

"You mean, you don't actually shoot the close-ups as I'm doing the commercial?"

"This must be your first job," Tony said.

Kelly blushed. "Is it that obvious?"

"That's okay, sweetheart—ask questions, that's what I'm here for."

"Well, then, if I wanted to—"

"Not now, doll. Let's go through the routine again, and watch your marks. Okay—ready."

They marched through the set two or three more times. Kelly thought it was a waste of time; she understood the action—she was a baby-sitter, getting a baby a bottle of milk.

"Now, you don't have much time for this bit," Tony continued, "so be quick about it. Let's keep it to ten seconds."

"Ten seconds?" It seemed awfully fast, but Kelly agreed. "Fine. But what about my dialogue—can I get it all in that fast?"

"You don't have to," Mona called. "There's no dialogue in this first bit."

"Too bad," Kelly said, secretly relieved not to have to worry about speaking as she followed Tony's choreography.

"No one told me," Tony complained.

"The creatives got together and did a rewrite this morning," Ray said. "The lines are all at the back-door shot now."

Tony turned in exasperation. "Randy," he complained, "the lines are all in the wave scene."

Lazily, Randy took a pipe out of his mouth. "That should speed things up. Get the rest of the talent on the set. Is the nurse here?"

"Yes," Mona said. "State law," she explained to Kelly. "With a two-year-old, you have to have a registered nurse on the set."

Kelly had been wondering where the baby was. Now Mona hurried toward a room at the back of the studio. A door opened, and a pleasant-looking woman came out, leading a toddler by the hand.

"Because of the child-labor laws," Mona told her, "the baby can only work two or three hours at a time."

Kelly checked the clock again—noontime. And if they could only shoot for three hours, she had nothing to worry about. She'd be done in plenty of time to make the track meet. She held a hand over her stomach to quiet the butterflies. Things were going smoothly enough, and she was only reasonably nervous. She was excited, and geared up, the way she felt before a big race—eager to get started, to show everyone what she could do.

"Ready, Kelly?" Tony asked.

She nodded brightly. "Let's do it!"

They brought the baby onto the set. "Samantha," the mother said, "this is Kelly. She's a very *nice* girl and she's going to be your *baby-sitter*."

Samantha stared at her.

"Mommy's just going to put you in this nice high chair—okay, sweetie? And we'll give you your very *favorite* peaches to eat!" An assistant appeared with a bowl of baby food and a delicate silver spoon. "Now the nice baby-sitter is going to watch you!"

Kelly took her place next to the high chair, giving Samantha her best I'm-your-friendly-baby-sitter look. Samantha dug her spoon into the strained peaches, ignoring everyone around her.

"Now Mommy's going to sit down over here and watch—all right?"

Samantha's big eyes widened as her mother walked to a folding chair next to the camera and sat down.

"Mommy?" the little girl said.

"Mommy's right here," her mother answered.

"Places, everybody," Tony called. Immediately, everyone on the set stopped what they were doing. Kelly put a hand to her stomach, which suddenly fluttered.

"Nice and easy, now, Kelly," Randy called. "Ready, and . . . action!"

For a split second, Kelly panicked. Did she feed Samantha?—no, she simply walked behind the table to the refrigerator. . . . She found the baby bottle and turned, walking back to the baby. She stopped—was she supposed to put the bottle down on the high chair, hand it to Samantha, or what?

"Cut," Randy yelled, just like in the movies. "Okay, everyone. Kelly—a little faster, and remember, turn *toward* the camera after you close the refrigerator door."

Kelly flushed. "Sorry. . . . I forgot. I'll get it . . ."

"Excuse me." The mother waved to get Randy's attention. "Randy, dear—don't you think this young lady should *look* at Samantha as she crosses? Sam is such an *adorable* girl, I know a *real* sitter would pay more attention."

Randy looked bored. "Glance at the baby," he told Kelly brusquely.

"Places—" Tony called again. This time, Kelly made the turn the right way, but Samantha threw her spoon over the side of the high chair, and they had to stop in the middle of the action.

The mother came running. "Oh, Samantha, are you all right?"

"Mrs. Evans," Randy said impatiently, "we have people here to check wardrobe and talent."

"Yes, but Samantha responds best to me!"

Kelly was beginning to realize just how hard it would be to get everything right. They did eight more takes before everything went smoothly, and then they shot eight more to see if they couldn't get it better. It was almost two o'clock.

"That's a wrap," Tony finally called. "Next setup."

Mrs. Evans grabbed Samantha as if rescuing her from danger. "Samantha has never caused extra takes," she told Tony. "When she has someone good to work with, that is," she added, glancing meaningfully at Kelly. "Amateurs throw off her timing."

"Timing?" Kelly glanced at Jennifer, hoping she didn't put *that* in her notes. "What kind of timing could a two-year-old have?"

"Some children are born with it."

Jennifer met Kelly's eyes after Mrs. Evans had left the set. "Some people are born with it," Kelly said, imitating Mrs. Evans's high-handed manner. "Don't you want to strangle her? And I would if I didn't have to make it to the meet on time."

"Oh, Kelly, I really think you should forget about the meet."

"But I can make it," Kelly insisted. "I know I can."

"Kelly," Tony interrupted, "we're set to do your close-up now. You've just spotted your boyfriend at the back door—you look up, smile, big wave—got it?"

"Look up, smile, wave," Kelly said. The only trouble was, she was staring at a big, empty camera lens—not at some boy's face.

"Hey, pretend it's Eric," Jennifer called.

Tony looked annoyed that Jennifer had dared to speak, but Mona nodded. "Is that your boyfriend?"

"Sort of." Kelly gave an embarrassed grin.

"Good—if it helps, think of the camera as Eric," Mona said.

Feeling foolish, Kelly stared into the lens. If she tried, she could almost see Eric's face in its polished surface—grinning at her, his eyes lighting up the way they did when he was pleased at something—as if he wanted to say all was forgiven between them. . . .

"Perfect," Randy called. "Do it just that way! Your expression is absolutely priceless!"

"Let's try a more flattering angle," Tony suggested. "She's a bit wide through the cheeks."

Wide? Kelly had always heard that her high cheekbones were one of her biggest assets as a model.

"Tilt your head to the right, sweetheart," Randy instructed.

Dutifully, Kelly posed, craning her neck. "It's a little awkward," she said politely. "Wouldn't it be easier to move the camera?"

Tony and Randy exchanged amused glances. "Just follow directions," Tony said in that same condescending manner. Kelly was flustered, but it was silly to let them bother her. This was more like the kind of modeling she was used to—she'd show them she deserved her growing reputation as a fine professional. She had talent and she would use it.

"How's this?" Her shoulder already ached from the difficult position.

"Good, good," Randy murmured, adjusting his camera. She heard the motor cranking film through the magazine.

"Don't freeze on us," Randy warned. "Keep the expression alive—that's better—no, no! Don't change the pose." He sighed. "Let's try it again. Remember, sweetheart—this is *film*, not *print*. You can't hold a pose like a dummy. Keep your eyes sparkling, hold the expression—but don't move!"

After the fourth take, Randy said they could shoot the wave scene.

Kelly concentrated on smiling brightly, ignoring the crimp in her neck as she waved.

"A little slow," Tony said, consulting a stopwatch. "I'll talk you through it. Ready . . . and . . ."

Kelly imagined Eric again—catching sight of her as she ran onto the field this afternoon.

"Look up—smile," Tony instructed. She flashed a bright smile, almost feeling her eyes light up with excitement as her imaginary Eric held his arms out to her. . . . "Now, wave—hold it—cut!"

Kelly dropped her hand.

"Don't let your hand flop around," Randy said patiently. "Try to make the motion sharp, crisp." He demonstrated.

"I know how to wave," she snapped, glancing anxiously at her watch. She was running out of time! This time, she gave a smart, military salute.

"How was that?"

"Perfect," Randy said with obvious relief. "Let's try it again."

It may have been perfect, but still they shot her again and again, smiling and waving. Her smile began to feel forced and frozen; she was sure her eyes were glazed. The hot lights made her perspire, and the makeupman constantly dashed onto the set to fluff loose powder onto her face to absorb the shine. Randy seemed pleased, but it was hardly the opportunity for real acting that Kelly had been waiting for.

"Let's keep up the momentum, people," Tony called. "Let's go right on to the dialogue shot."

Kelly felt a thrill of fear and anticipation—the dialogue, her big chance to shine.

At that moment, another baby suddenly appeared on the set—Samantha's twin.

"We often use twins," Mona told Kelly. "We get twice the work done that way."

"This is Jessica, Samantha's sister," Mrs. Evans crooned. Jessica fussed and whimpered. "It's all these strange people," the mother said anxiously.

"Oh, don't worry, I'm terrific with babies." Kelly tickled Jessica's tummy, cooing softly. Jessica's face screwed up and she began to wail.

"She *hates* being tickled," her mother cried. "Now look what you've done! She's very sensitive."

"I never heard of a baby who didn't like to be tickled," Kelly protested.

"This one doesn't," Mrs. Evans fumed. Mona rushed to the mother's side.

"Now, now," she said, trying to calm both mother and child. "Let's just relax—everything is fine. . . ."

"That girl is impossible," Mrs. Evans sputtered. "Look, now she's upset my baby!"

Kelly could barely hold her temper. "I'm impossible? Look, Mrs. Evans, it's hot under these lights, I'm getting a terrible headache, and I have lines to remember, but I know how to do my job. And your baby might quiet down faster if you stopped hovering over her."

"I think I know my own daughter." Mrs. Evans reached for a bottle of orange juice and began feeding it to Jessica. "Poor baby," she crooned.

Mona shot Kelly a warning glance. "Jessica is a *wonderful baby*," she assured Jessica's mother. "Of course you know best. She's calmer already. Let's get her on the set." To Kelly she added, "And no tickling this time."

"No tickling," Jennifer recited, dutifully recording the scene. "The Drama Club is going to love this."

"You don't have to write down *everything*," Kelly said crankily.

"I have to write something."

"I told you, Jen, write about the real acting."

"You mean this isn't real acting?"

Kelly glowered. "This is a take, Jennifer. You don't kid around on a set during a real take." Quickly, Kelly ran through her lines, hoping the distractions hadn't made her forget anything. "Balmour's has casuals for everybody's baby . . ."

"That's good," Tony called. "Keep it at just that speed and we'll wrap in no time."

The crew adjusted the lights once more, and then Randy signaled for baby Jessica to be placed in Kelly's arms. You could almost hear the tension as everyone waited to see how Jessica would react.

"That's a good girl," Kelly cooed nervously at the baby. "You're a pretty girl." To her relief, Jessica smiled up at her, quite happy with her "baby-sitter."

"Wonderful!" Tony called. The Balmour's people smiled and clapped each other on the shoulders. Kelly took her mark on the set.

"Ready . . . and action!" Tony called.

This is it! My big moment—Kelly Blake's acting debut!

"Balmour's has casuals . . . Oh!" Calmly, Jessica spit up frothy orange juice onto Kelly's white outfit. "Oh . . ." She glanced helplessly at the camera. "Uh, casuals . . ."

"Cut!"

Instantly, Kelly was surrounded. Mona screamed for Patsy, and the stylist came running. "Take that dress right off," she cried.

Oh, no—just when everything was finally going right!

Patsy practically stripped the spotted dress off Kelly, frantic that the orange juice might leave a stain. Even Ray and Anita crowded into the dressing room, as if the spill was the biggest disaster they'd ever seen.

"It's going . . ." Patsy reported. Everyone seemed to have stopped breathing. "It's out!"

Ray and Anita actually cheered.

"I know," Jennifer piped up. "Why don't you use this blow dryer on it, to get the wet out?"

"That is a wonderful idea," Patsy cried, and she bent down and gave Jennifer a big kiss on the cheek.

The blow dryer did its job, Kelly's hair and makeup were retouched, and the clock struck four—no time left if she was to make the meet at all, and Kelly hadn't gotten anywhere in terms of showing off her acting. But the crew had to recheck the lights, and the propman rearranged his bowl of fruit.

"I thought we'd be finished by three," Kelly cried.

Mona looked at Kelly in disbelief. "Who told you that, the commercial fairy?"

"But I have to be somewhere afterward," Kelly said.

"You have to be *here*," Mona said firmly. "Whatever you're worried about, forget it. There's a lot of money invested in this spot already. Just concentrate on your lines."

Tony rubbed his hands together. "This is your big moment, Kelly. Randy—you ready?"

Randy relit his pipe and inhaled luxuriously. "Anytime."

Kelly took a deep breath. *No time to worry about the meet right now—time to concentrate. Get the right feeling, the right attitude.*

"Just say your lines normally, sweetheart," Randy said, strolling into position behind the camera.

"I know. I've got it. I'm ready."

"And forget I'm here," he instructed. "Look at the red light and your eyes will be focused in the right place. Can you remember that?"

Of course I can remember! "Yes, yes," she exclaimed. "I remember. I can do it! Let's go!"

"Camera rolling."

She cocked her head to one side, flashed a high smile and willed her eyes to light up with enthusiasm. "Balmour's has casuals," she began. Jessica hiccuped.

Cut!

"Balmour's casuals have . . ."

Cut!

She had flubbed the lines. Jessica started to drool, and Mrs. Evans sprang onto the set, fussing, while Patsy sprang at Kelly's dress, wiping it quickly with a towel. It was getting later and later.

"Balmour's has casuals for—"

"Hold it," Ray interrupted. "Let's put the stress on *casuals*—what do you think, Anita?"

Anita agreed, and Randy directed Kelly to stress the word *casuals*.

"Balmour's has *casuals* for everybody's baby . . ."

"Again," Randy ordered.

Kelly shifted Jessica to a more comfortable position. The baby was getting heavier and heavier and her back ached from the weight. Under her collar, a damp spot where the baby had drooled was starting to chafe terribly. It was getting hard to concentrate.

"Balmour's casuals are busy . . ."

"Again!" Randy called patiently. The headache began to pound behind Kelly's eyes.

"*Balmour's* has casuals . . ."

"Stress on *casuals*," Tony cried.

Her back was absolutely breaking, but she tried to put enthusiasm in her voice one more time. "Balmour's has *casuals* for *every*body's baby . . ."

"Cut! Try to remember what Randy told you," Tony said impatiently. He repeated the line with Kelly: "Balmour's has *casuals* . . ."

". . . and ready and action!"

Kelly took a deep breath. "Balmour's has . . ." Jessica hiccuped loudly, and Kelly, feeling the strain, began to giggle.

"Again!"

"Balmour's has cas . . . Balmour's has cas . . . Balmour's has casuals for every busy baby. Every busybody. Every . . . Balmour's has contempt for anybody's baby!" She dissolved into a helpless fit of the giggles, nearly dropping Jessica (who felt as heavy as a baby elephant at this point) right onto her Pampered bottom.

There was deadly quiet in the studio.

"What did you say?" Randy took his pipe out of his mouth.

Kelly stifled a hiccuping bleat of laughter. "I . . . I think I said, 'Balmour's has casual contempt for busybodies . . .'" She choked, wiping her eyes. "I don't know what I said. I just got the giggles so bad." She took a deep breath. "I'm all right now. I have it straight." She composed her face, picturing an image of the way the Balmour's Girl ought to look, and looked up, expecting smiling faces. Instead she was met by a silence that felt almost like the air before a thunderstorm, heavy and threatening. Her smile faded.

Mrs. Evans stepped up and whisked Jessica out of Kelly's arms, as if Kelly were suddenly untouchable.

"What's the matter with everyone? It wasn't on purpose." Kelly glanced at Jennifer, expecting

her to be sympathetic. Hadn't they made up the
phony lines together?

"Do you think this is a joke, young lady?" Ray's
face, beet-red and sweaty under the lights,
almost made Kelly laugh, but she bit her lip.

"No, of course not."

"Then do you think you could wipe that smile
off your face?"

Incredulous, Kelly stared at him. "I'm not
smiling. I told you, I'm sorry. It was just nerves.
Really, Randy, Mona, everyone, I am sorry. I'm
fine now." She took another deep breath.
"There—all set. Okay, let's try it again."

"This isn't a high-school study hall, young
woman." Ray's face was getting even redder. He
looked as if he might explode.

Mona's voice was low and calm. "I'm terribly
sorry," she said to Ray and Anita. "It is hot in
here, and it has been a long day."

"Not that long."

"She didn't mean anything. She's new at this.
It's her first job."

"First job or not, I will *not* stand for that
attitude."

"Maybe," Anita said, "you should have hired a
girl with more experience."

"We're all doing the best we can."

"If you call that her best, maybe we should find
someone else."

Kelly stared as Ray and Anita argued with
Mona. Were they talking about her? *But*, she
wanted to protest, *I have natural acting ability.
I could be a great star!*

Nine

Randy and Tony left their cameras, the soundman and propman pulled out cigarettes and lit
up, and everyone in the studio acted as if the
workday were over.

Mona, her features grave, faced Kelly.

"You're not doing another take."

Quietly, Jennifer closed her notebook.

"What?" Kelly saw Mona's lips move, she heard
her speak—but she couldn't quite connect herself
to the words Mona was saying. She shook her
head. "No take? You mean we're taking a break?"

Mona simply looked at her. "No break. Let's
go, Kelly," she said quietly.

"Go? Go where?"

Kelly glanced at Jennifer, but her friend's eyes
were downcast. It was impossible to see her
expression.

"Look, we'll send your pay voucher to the

agency. I'll sign you out for five o'clock, a full day's rate, okay?"

"Wait—I don't understand. Are we going to finish the shoot tomorrow?"

Mona's lips were pursed. "Kelly, you're not going to finish the shoot at all."

"Not at all?" Kelly's mouth went dry. Her hands got hot and flushed and tingly.

"I'm not sure I understand," she said weakly. "Don't you want to see me do the scene?"

"Look, honey, Ray and Anita think they want a different image after all. And . . . someone with more dialogue experience."

"But you said at the audition I was good with dialogue."

"You've got a nice fresh approach," Mona said hastily, "very casual, and nice, but—maybe this particular job calls for a little more experience than we realized."

"Experience?" With a sinking sensation, Kelly looked at Jennifer, who was pretending very hard not to be listening. "Look, Mona." She lowered her voice. "I got a little confused, a little tongue-tied. I know the dialogue. Balmour's has casuals . . . I was just a little nervous before. . . ."

Mona began to look very uncomfortable. "It isn't your delivery"—she paused, groping for words—"it's, uh, your *presence* isn't exactly what we thought it would be."

"Presence?" Perplexed, Kelly tried again. "Mona, I know I shouldn't have laughed like that, but it was just nerves. They're not upset because of the lines I said, are they? It was just a stupid joke, you know, a play on words, nothing serious. I don't think Balmour's has contempt for anyone!"

She searched Mona's face in disbelief. "They didn't think I was serious, did they?"

Mona spoke stiffly. "There really isn't anything to joke about."

"But I—I wasn't making fun of anything, I was just tense." She couldn't seem to stop herself from pleading too hard, making it worse.

"I'm always kidding around like that. See, we made up those lines, Jennifer and me, as a joke, it didn't mean anything. Tell her, Jen . . ."

"I'm afraid these people didn't see it as a joke," Mona stated flatly.

Tears welled up in Kelly's eyes. Her voice cracked. "I can't believe this is happening to me. This is supposed to be my big moment, everyone's waiting to hear all about it." She grasped Mona's arm, but Mona pried her hand loose.

"I'm sorry, but we just don't want you, Kelly," Mona said firmly. "There's no point in crying about it. You'll only make it worse for yourself. Leave the dress on the hook in the dressing room."

Kelly made one last try. "I can do the job, I know I can."

"It isn't a disgrace." Mona walked away.

But it *was* a disgrace, a total disgrace. Behind her, Kelly heard Ray and Anita arguing with Randy and Mona. She brushed past Jennifer, knocking her friend's notebook to the floor.

"She was all wrong," she heard Anita say. "Maybe we need someone, I don't know, more unusual."

"Yes, yes—unusual," Ray gushed. "Exotic. How about this other little girl? This girl right here?"

Kelly heard Jennifer's startled voice. "Me? I'm not a model—or an actress."

"Oh, she's a doll," Mona said, "but—"

Ray interrupted. "I like her, so what's the problem?"

"She's not a pro, Ray," Mona insisted. Anita cut her off. "Who is she? If she's right for Balmour's . . ."

"But I'm not . . ." Jennifer said.

Kelly's ears burned. They wanted Jennifer to replace her! Jennifer, a total unknown, a complete amateur—it was too much to bear.

She fled to the dressing room, pulling off the horrible dress, which mussed her hair. Automatically she reached for a brush, then realized she didn't have to worry about her hair—no one would be taking her picture anymore today. She threw on her jeans, her sweater, her coat, grabbed her bag, and burst from the room.

In the studio, Ray was holding his hand over Jennifer's head as if measuring her height. Kelly bolted for the front door. She thought she heard someone calling her name, but she didn't want to see any of those terrible people again. They were shallow, self-indulgent—the awful mother, the spoiled babies. . . . They were pitiful, that's what—she pitied them!

Making commercials was a horrible business. She would never take a job to do another commercial as long as she lived!

At the corner she tried to hail a cab. Some boys in the playground across the street noticed her and began whistling, hooting, and teasing as she stood there, praying for a cab to stop. Two or three of the boys pretended to climb the playground fence after her, hurling themselves against the chain links, rattling the metal. She took off, running across the avenue, ignoring the honking horns and the yells of drivers. The streets were full of high-school boys heading home from school, and it seemed as though every one of them had a choice remark to hurl at her as she ran along the sidewalk, her tears running freely now. *I must look like a crazy person*, she thought. Finally, waiting at a crosswalk for the light to change, she spotted an empty cab and flagged it down. "Franklyn, New Jersey," she blurted.

The cab driver turned to stare at her. "That's gonna be an expensive ride," he said suspiciously.

She dug in her purse, pulled out all her money, and waved it in his face. "I'll pay it—just get me there, and hurry!"

When Judith Blake opened the front door in response to the door bell, she looked startled to see Kelly, tearstained and weary, standing with a cab driver.

"I'm afraid we need some more cab fare, ma'am," he said politely.

"Pay him, Mom." Kelly handed her mother her wallet and dragged herself into the living room, sinking into the comfort and safety of the over-stuffed sofa.

"Well . . . just a minute . . ." Mrs. Blake hurried to her purse, pulling out the remainder of the fare.

"Think she had a rough day, ma'am," the cabbie suggested. He tipped his hat toward Kelly in the living room, and she lifted a hand limply in reply.

"Thank you," Mrs. Blake said uncertainly, closing the door behind him. She stepped into the living room.

"What is going on?" she said.

"Don't ask."

"You look exhausted—but a cab from Manhattan—I thought you and Jennifer would come home on the bus."

There were voices in the hall, and Tina and her father appeared, arguing over a catalog of camping gear that Tina was campaigning to buy.

"Kelly, how'd it go?" Tina flung herself onto the sofa. "How's the big TV star?"

"You look beat," Mr. Blake said cheerfully. "You must've earned your money today. . . ."

A few more tears squeezed out of Kelly's eyes. She was surprised there were any left—she thought she was beyond tears.

"Why, honey, what's wrong?" Her mother watched her in concern. "Kelly took a cab home from the city," she told her husband.

"A cab!" Mr. Blake exploded. "From Manhattan? Are we millionaires?"

"I took care of it," Mrs. Blake said. "Honey, don't cry. You can tell me . . ."

"It was horrible, awful . . ."

"That cab must have cost thirty dollars," Mr. Blake said.

Mrs. Blake hushed him. "Kelly—what happened to Jennifer? Is she all right?"

"I don't know and I don't care. She's no friend of mine—I hope I never see her again."

Kelly's parents exchanged looks. "Tina," her mother said, nodding at the door.

"Oh, all right," Tina griped. "I've heard that

one before—Tina, leave the room. Tina, you're too young. So what—so they had some stupid fight. What's new about that?"

"Upstairs, Tina," her father warned.

"I know, it's none of my business—why don't you just say so?" Still grumbling, Tina left the room.

"Now let's have the story," Mrs. Blake said calmly.

"It was horrible . . ." Kelly choked. "The worst, most humiliating day of my life."

"It couldn't have been that bad," her mother said soothingly. "You're upset now, but we can straighten this out, whatever it is."

"You can't—it has nothing to do with you. It's just me. I've never been in this much trouble before. I—I got fired from the job."

Her mother gasped in alarm. "Fired! Oh, no, Kelly."

"Why?" her father asked.

"They said they wanted a different type. After I worked hard all day, then they changed their minds. They're not rational people, Dad, I mean it."

"It will work out all right," he said soothingly.

"All right!" Mrs. Blake exclaimed. "How can you say that, Hal? Kelly, what did Meg say?"

"I didn't call her—they said they would."

Her mother frowned. "You should call Meg yourself, honey. You'll have to face her sometime."

"No, I won't. They said they'd pay for my time, so Meg doesn't need explanations. Please, it's bad enough as it is—don't you 'see, I'm finished with the FLASH! agency."

"At least you don't have to worry about getting paid," her father said.

"Hal, this is serious," her mother said. "This is Kelly's career we're talking about."

Kelly's head was throbbing. She pressed her hands to her temples.

"Honey," her mother said, "are you feeling all right? You look flushed. You're not coming down with something, are you?"

"I sort of feel like I'm getting a cold—the cab ride, I guess. The window was open . . ."

"In this weather! You get right into a hot tub! This is no time to play around with your health. You're always vulnerable to illness when you're feeling low."

"I do feel a little sick to my stomach," Kelly said, surprised that it seemed true the minute she said it. "I don't feel well at all."

Mrs. Blake laid a cool palm against Kelly's forehead. "A hot tub and right to bed," she ordered. "I'll bring you up a tray later."

"Bed sounds wonderful." Gratefully, Kelly dragged herself up the stairs.

Tina poked her head into the bedroom fifteen minutes later. "Jennifer called while you were in the tub," she announced. "She said she'd call back in half an hour."

"When she does, tell her I'm napping," Kelly snapped, reaching around to fluff up her pillows.

"You look wide awake to me," Tina said. "Why won't you talk to her?"

"I don't want to, that's why."

"Well, if I knew what had happened, I'd know what to tell her."

Kelly eyed her sister suspiciously. "Didn't Jennifer fill you in?"

"She didn't say anything, except to ask for you. When I tell her you're *napping*, should I say you'll call back?"

"Maybe when I feel better," Kelly said vaguely.

Mrs. Blake came in with Kelly's supper tray—soup and toast and applesause. "Tina, don't bother your sister," she warned.

"Okay." Tina sighed. "But I wish someone around here would tell me something."

Kelly sat up and dipped her spoon into the hot soup. It tasted delicious.

"Was that about Jennifer calling?" Mrs. Blake brushed the hair off Kelly's forehead.

"I guess."

"Why won't you talk to her—can't you tell me?"

"I don't want to talk about any of it. Not the commercial, nothing—the whole experience was too terrible. You don't know what those people were like! The baby's mother was a horrible person, and the baby threw up on me, and Randy and Tony bossed me around, and it got on my nerves, but I tried—I tried so hard! And I said the lines again and again," she finished, "trying to get them exactly right—and then, after all that, they told me I wasn't the right type and they fired me!"

"For no reason?" Her mother looked skeptical. "They must have had more explanation than that."

"Well, the only thing I can think of," Kelly confessed uneasily, "is just that—well, right at the very end, I made a little joke."

"What kind of a joke?"

"Well . . . things were tense and everyone

was tired, and I said one of the lines Jen and I'd made up." She shrugged. "I forget exactly— something about Balmour's being expensive. 'Balmour's has contempt for anybody's baby . . .'"

"Well, they *are* extremely expensive," Mrs. Blake said indignantly.

"I know!" Kelly sat up straighter, relieved that her mother was sympathetic. "And it was just a silly joke, but they went completely crazy. The Balmour's lady flipped out and the ad agency people flipped out. You'd think I'd started a war or something!"

"They don't sound very professional," her mother said. "One little joke. Don't they know how kids are?"

"They don't," Kelly said eagerly. "That's exactly it. They said they wanted me to relax and be myself, be a normal, ordinary kid. But when I did, they jumped all over me! And then"—she could hardly bring herself to admit it—"then I heard them offering *Jennifer* my part."

"Jennifer!" Her mother was startled. "Jennifer? She's no model! And no actress, either."

"And no friend of mine," Kelly said hotly.

"Well, I don't believe it. Why would they give Jennifer a job like that? She has no experience."

"Can you imagine how I feel, knowing my best friend is a traitor? How could she do this to me? I was never so humiliated in my life. She stood there enjoying it while they told me how terrible I was, lusting after my job. I don't understand it, I really don't."

"I don't, either," her mother said. "Jennifer isn't stagestruck. I can't imagine her wanting your job. Although . . . it must have been hard for her when you started modeling. All the attention you get, and the glamour, and you don't see her as much as you used to. Maybe she was jealous of you."

Kelly snorted. "And now, Jennifer Lee is shooting *my* commercial, taking *my* job. She was jealous, all right! I didn't know how jealous. I never want to talk to her again. She's a traitor, a phony, and a backstabber."

"Now, Kelly, you don't know what really happened after you left."

"I know she was no help. She didn't say it was *her* line about Balmour's. She let me take the blame."

"I doubt they cared who made up the line."

"I care. That's not the way a true friend acts. I trusted Jen, and she let me down."

"Well—things will look better in the morning," her mother said. "There's no use dwelling on it now. I can see why you're mad at Jennifer, but, well, it'll work itself out. Right now you get some sleep. You've got school tomorrow."

School. How could she face school? How was she supposed to talk to the Drama Club about acting when she'd been fired? She'd be a laughing stock. Julie Higgins, Patty Berg, they'd never forgive her. And then there was the track team. She'd let them down, too . . . Eric . . . Coach . . .

"I don't know about school," she said uneasily. "I don't feel too well."

Mrs. Blake laid her hand over Kelly's forehead. "We'll see how you feel in the morning. Now sleep."

Kelly sighed. Her soft pillow and warm sheets

felt wonderful. "Okay," she murmured. "Sleep would be good. Good night, Mom."

"Kelly"— her mother hesitated in the doorway—"didn't you say something about a track meet today? Or was that another day?"

"Another day," Kelly said hastily. There was no use going into *that* right now.

Mrs. Blake smiled. "Get some sleep."

Ten

Kelly stretched pleasantly and thought about staying in bed all weekend. *A good rest really helps,* she thought. *Even Mom noticed how much better I look. Good thing she let me stay home from school yesterday.*

The novel she'd been reading slipped to the floor, and as she bent to pick it up there was a knock at the door—*Tina again.*

"What is it?" Kelly said crankily. "What do you want?"

"Hi—your mom said you were feeling better today."

"Sue!" Kelly started guiltily as the tall girl entered her bedroom. "Sue Levine! Oh . . . didn't my mom tell you I'm sick . . . ?"

"Yeah—everyone knows, that's why I came." Sue hesitated, then sat on the desk chair, across the room. "I haven't been over in a long time. You have such a nice room, Kelly. Really cozy."

"Yeah, thanks." Kelly managed to straighten the covers around her as well as smooth her hair back hastily. "Why the visit? Aren't you afraid I'm contagious?" She laughed at her own joke, hoping Sue wouldn't notice how uneasy a visit from the girls' track captain made her.

"I came to bring you this." Sue fished in her purse, her long honey-colored bangs flopping into her eyes. Kelly could never understand how Sue could run with that fringe of hair in her face, but long bangs were Sue's trademark. Since she kept the rest of her hair cropped short in the interest of speed and efficiency, she called the bangs her "feminine indulgence."

"You brought me a newspaper?"

"A paper, and a special card. Open it up."

Kelly tore the top off the envelope. On the card, a steam engine puffed out a cloud of smoke. "Get Well Soon!" the cloud said. On the inside, the engine puffed up a mountain. "We're running out of steam without you!"

All the girls and boys on the track teams had signed their names.

"This is great, Sue, thanks—I didn't expect to be missed. Especially since my dad told me you guys beat the socks off Edison without me."

"We ran a great meet, but we could have done even better if you'd been there. You must feel terrible that you missed it. Eric told us all how much you'd wanted to compete."

"I really did," Kelly said, feeling guilty. "I feel awful about letting everyone down. Especially Eric—he thought I had real team spirit."

"You can't help it if you're sick," Sue said sensibly, reminding Kelly of Jennifer.

Kelly sighed. "I'm not sure Coach believed me when I told him I had the flu that's going around. But I promise, Sue—from now on, I'll be the team's most conscientious runner. I'll really make it up to you. I've decided to rededicate myself to the team and concentrate more on high school and friends than modeling. After all, I'll have plenty of time for a career, but high school only comes once."

Sue grinned and punched Kelly in the arm. "That's the old Kelly Blake talking! But, really, you aren't thinking of giving up modeling, are you? Especially not now—you're about to become a star! Everyone's excited about your commercial and your talk to the Drama Club."

"Didn't Jennifer tell you?" Kelly said.

"Tell me what?"

"Oh, nothing," Kelly said evasively. She coughed several times. "Just that I may have to cancel my talk if this flu doesn't get better."

"Oh, they'll wait for you, don't worry. Are you kidding? Everyone's dying to hear about your big acting success, especially me. You know"—Sue leaned forward—"I was kind of surprised you kept up with track this semester. I figured your career would be more important, but it's terrific the way you've stayed on the team. I really admire you."

"I wanted to do both."

"It can't be easy. You know, if you'd missed the meet because of your commercial, no one would've blamed you."

"They wouldn't?" Kelly flushed.

"Well, especially not since we won," Sue said cheerfully. "But that's the way things go—if we'd lost the meet, some kids might've blamed you for not showing. But it's dumb to talk about it now. You're sick, and we won, so it doesn't really matter."

"You mean I'm off the hook," Kelly said grimly.

"You could say that. But why worry? You just try to get well for the Drama Club speech. Julie has everyone so excited about it—that will make up for your missing the meet."

It'll make up for it all right—when everyone finds out there isn't a commercial anymore! But why hasn't Jennifer told the truth?

"By the way, Sue," Kelly said as casually as possible, "did you happen to mention to Jennifer that you were coming over here?" Kelly looked at her get-well card, keeping her eyes down to hide her anxious expression.

"Yes, and I guess she'll be here to see you later. Your best friend is bound to come over when you're not feeling well."

Ex-best friend, Kelly thought. "Jen was there when . . . when I got sick, you know. During the commercial shoot. She didn't mention that?"

"Um," Sue said vaguely, searching through the newspaper for the sports section. "What did you say, Kelly? No, Jennifer didn't mention the commercial. I guess she doesn't want to spoil your talk. Oh, here it is—speaking of stars, take a look at this!"

Eric Powers's face stared up at them. "Track Star Leads Team to Rousing Victory," the headline said.

"What a great picture!"

"I thought you might like to keep it," Sue said slyly.

Kelly flushed. "Thanks. I wouldn't have seen it. I forgot all about today's sports section."

Actually, she had avoided the paper when her father offered it to her, too guilty about missing the meet to read details of the team's success. "This article really raves about Eric!"

"He's some guy, isn't he?" Sue said. "I really like him. He's not like most of the jocks around here, real impressed with themselves—I hate people like that. Speaking of which, you should have seen Julie Higgins and Patty Berg hanging all over Eric at the party for the team last night. Julie's been trying to get a date with him all year, but I think he sees through her. She only wants him because he's more interested in you, and Julie's jealous because you're not part of her snobby crowd."

"Not because I didn't want to be," Kelly pointed out. "Before I started modeling, Julie and Patty didn't know I was alive."

"So what's stopping you now?"

"I'm not sure. My old friends, like Lisa and Rochelle, will never belong to that clique. But it's tempting. I've never been in *the* group before."

"And Eric is sort of in with them. He goes to their parties, doesn't he?"

"Yes," Kelly admitted. "Hey, Sue, do me a favor—look and see if Eric's car is back in his driveway."

"No, it's not there."

Kelly frowned. "He's been out all morning. And he was out late last night, too." Maybe it was her guilty conscience, but she longed for some reassurance that Eric still liked her.

"He was celebrating our victory," Sue said. "But I'm sure he would've had more fun if you'd been there, so don't worry. I'm sure he's not interested in anyone else."

Kelly hesitated. That wasn't exactly the truth. "Sue, there's something I'd like to talk about, and you're the only one who might really be able to help."

"What is it?"

"No one in school knows this, except Jennifer, so you can see how important it is to keep it between us. But . . ."

"You look upset. Maybe you'd better tell me—I won't spread anything around."

"I know you won't. See, it's about having a long-distance romance. How do you and your boyfriend work things out?"

"It's not easy. Kerry is great, but it's a tough situation, anyway. I never know when he might meet some college girl more interesting than me. I don't see him very often lately, and on top of it all, being Kerry's girl stops me from getting more involved with groups at school. Every weekend I can, I visit him."

"Well, my problem is sort of the opposite." Kelly took a deep breath. "Eric is still going out with his old girlfriend, from Ohio. It's really complicated, because their families are close friends and they still visit each other. She has this hold on Eric, even though he's said he likes me and I know he'd go with me if it weren't for her. Oh please, Sue, don't tell anyone else about this, I'd die. Please don't let this out."

"Relax. You can count on me. I know how much that can hurt, and I won't tell anyone." She sighed. "But I don't have any great advice, either. People aren't very honorable sometimes— lots of girls at Kerry's school know about me, but that doesn't stop them from flirting with him. I just have to trust him and hope our relationship is special enough to survive."

"That's just it—you had a chance to have a special relationship before Kerry went away to school. But Eric and I are just beginning ours, and there's Rissa, smack in the middle of it! You must know some way I can eliminate the competition."

"I don't," Sue said sadly, shaking her head. "I don't know any way to do that."

"I've been playing hard to get, hoping Eric would realize he likes me around. And also because Rissa is so demanding that I thought he'd be relieved to be with a girl who's easygoing."

"Sounds like a good plan," Sue said. "But don't overdo it. Playing hard to get is risky. Eric could get the wrong signals and think you're not very interested."

"You're right. And making him jealous won't work, either. I know that already." Kelly sighed.

"Kerry always said I made him feel so special that he started feeling that way about me. I don't know if holding back your feelings ever works. Whenever I get worried that Kerry might find someone else, I try to remember what he said."

"I didn't realize it was so hard on you, Sue. I'm sorry I brought it up. Anyway, you *are* special, so you shouldn't worry about Kerry." Sue's face lit up in pleasure.

"You really think so? It helps to hear that."

It helps you, Kelly thought, *but who's going to help me?* She stared at the house across the street. If miracles existed, Eric's car would drive up right now—he'd look up at Kelly's window, wave, and everything would be all right again.

Kelly stared harder, but nothing happened. Maybe miracles didn't happen anymore.

"Well," Sue said, "so much for boy trouble."

"Sure, let's talk about something else." Kelly tried not to show her distress. If Sue couldn't think of anything positive to say, then the situation was hopeless. Maybe she'd already played *too* hard to get—and if she had, then she might just as well give up completely.

Eleven

"Here's a snack," Tina said, carrying a tray into Kelly's bedroom. She plopped the tray onto Kelly's knees so abruptly that the plate of fresh-baked cookies and pot of tea slid into each other. "How's the invalid? Having fun with all your visitors?"

"Ow, Tina—watch out." Kelly straightened the tray, lifting it higher on the bed. "Sue is the only one who's visited."

Tina watched as Kelly devoured the cookies. "You're about as sick as I am."

"I'm really not feeling well," Kelly said indignantly. "You're a very unsympathetic person, Tina. It's a nasty trait."

It was funny; she'd lied about having the flu, but she really did feel awful. Not achy or feverish, the way she usually felt with the flu, but awful, nonetheless, when she thought of the Drama Club meeting looming ahead of her.

"I'm sympathetic," Tina protested. "I just don't think you're sick. Except lovesick, over Eric."

Kelly glanced at Tina with a rueful expression. "Yeah—so much for playing hard to get," she said miserably. "What's the saying—fight fire with fire? If Eric likes silly clinging females like Prissy Rissy, I guess I should've acted helpless and fragile, too. Oh, well, too late now."

Tina made a face. "Ugh—I couldn't stand it if you acted that way. And you'd hate yourself!"

"I'm not so sure." Kelly stared mournfully at the newspaper Sue had left. "At least I'd have Eric."

"Maybe, but I think you should be yourself and let Eric see what he's missing."

"Sisters must think alike, Tina—that was my plan, but it doesn't seem to be working."

Tina watched as Kelly poured herself a cup of tea. "Meg Dorian called again. Aren't you ever going to speak to her?"

"When I'm better." Kelly evaded Tina's stare. "It's not polite to watch someone eat," she said haughtily.

"If I were you, I wouldn't lie around in bed. I'd be scared Meg would find another model to replace me. You're not that special, you know."

"It so happens I don't care that much about modeling. I never did. It's not the only career there is in the world."

"It's the only thing you can do right now that pays so much money," Tina pointed out. "You're not supersmart, like Jennifer—you won't win any scholarships. How are you ever going to help pay for college if you don't model?"

Kelly used her most cutting tone of voice. "Did anyone ever tell you you're not normal? Try to remember this—you're a thirteen-year-old kid, not my mother."

"You tell me I'm not normal all the time," Tina answered. She shrugged. "I don't care."

Kelly pushed the tray away. "I could get a different job," she defended herself. "I'm not stupid. I'm not a brain like Jennifer, but I'm not stupid, either."

"Okay—what job?"

"Lots of things."

"Yeah, like, be a waitress, or work at a department store. Big deal."

"If I worked very hard and studied, I might get a scholarship to some college."

Tina was unimpressed. "You'll have to do something—Mom and Dad'll kill you if you don't go."

It was true—her parents were definite about that. Kelly was going to college; she was going to have opportunities neither Hal nor Judith Blake ever had. Before Kelly began modeling, her mother had often talked about getting herself a job as soon as Tina was older, to help put away money. Lately she hadn't mentioned it at all. It was as if she were counting on Kelly's modeling fees to help the family.

Suppose Tina is right—suppose I save only pennies from some other part-time job, suppose I can't get a college scholarship. What then?

Of course, there was her *real* father—he had plenty of money. Kelly hadn't seen Johnny Edmonds in ten years, and he wasn't very reliable. Her mother always said that. Actually, to Kelly, Hal Blake felt more like her real father than

Johnny Edmonds ever had. That was hardly surprising, since her mother had divorced her father when Kelly was only eighteen months old, after realizing that her early marriage had been a terrible mistake. Hal Blake was the only father Kelly could ever remember having. She sighed; it was best not to count on help from Johnny Edmonds or anyone else.

She snapped angrily at Tina, "You really know how to cheer someone up. Thanks a lot."

Tina turned to leave. "By the way, you'd better fix your hair or something. It looks lousy."

"So—what do I care?"

"You'll care if Eric sees you looking like that."

"Well, he's not going to see me, is he? Really, Tina."

Tina shrugged. "Mom said he could see you. But maybe he'll go home instead."

"What are you talking about?"

"Nothing. Just that Eric is downstairs talking to Mom, and she said he could visit you for a few minutes, and I should tell you to straighten up in here . . ."

"Tina! I could kill you!" Kelly leapt from the bed, dashing to the bathroom to throw cold water on her face and get the tangles out of her hair. "Why didn't you tell me . . ."

"I just did tell you."

"Oh!" Kelly knocked Tina aside, scurrying back to the bedroom to throw her pretty blue robe over her pajamas. "You're impossible!"

"You move awfully fast for someone who's sick."

"Get out of here," Kelly hissed. "And take the tray with you." She plumped her pillows and smoothed the blankets. Sitting demurely in the bed, she picked up the newspaper and folded it to the sports section, assuming a calm expression.

Seconds later, there was a knock on the door and Eric poked his head inside.

"Eric—what a nice surprise!" She put the paper down.

"Hi—how are you feeling?" He was wearing a freshly ironed shirt and faded blue corduroys, carrying a gym bag over one shoulder. He really was adorable, though not exactly the type to be a male model.

"Oh, I'm much better. You know how the flu is . . . it comes and goes. I'm not contagious or anything," she quickly added.

Eric pulled the desk chair to the side of the bed. "I was sorry to hear you got sick. I, uh, I would've come over sooner, but the car—I've had it in the shop since yesterday. I just got it back."

"The shop!"

"The guys at Smiley's Garage are pretty nice. They promised the car for today, and they kept their promise. I have to admire that."

"Yeah, I admire people who keep promises," she said, ignoring her nagging conscience. "Tell me about the Edison meet. You're really a star— picture in the paper and everything."

"I had a good day. But the girls were the real stars. Edison has some really strong runners, like Cathy Bodner—fast, and great endurance, too. But Sue Levine is even better. I hadn't realized how much she's improved in the last few weeks. She's really good. Of course, you weren't there. You're faster than Sue, aren't you?"

"Yeah, on short distances."

"We had a great party last night—nothing fancy," he quickly reassured her. "Just the team and some other kids at Julie Higgins's, playing records, no big deal. I'm sorry you had to miss it, though. It was fun. Some of the kids are going to the double feature downtown tonight. It's too bad you're sick."

He was practically asking for a date, and she couldn't go! Why had she ever pretended to be sick! "I guess I'm missing a lot," she said. Maybe this was a good time to admit everything. "Uh, Eric . . . I'm not *that* sick. In fact, Thursday, at the shoot . . ."

"Hey, that must have been lots of fun."

"Not much. The baby spat up on me, and we did endless takes. Actually, everything went wrong. And at the end, when I was really anxious to be the big star and do my best acting"—she would tell him how it had *really* ended—"the funniest thing happened. . . ."

Eric looked at his watch. "Oh, no, I forgot all about Timmy! I was supposed to pick him up at his friend's house. I'd better get over there. Sorry to run. Maybe I'll come over tomorrow."

"That would be nice."

"Oh, I forgot. I can't. Timmy has some sort of scout thing. We'll be gone most of the day." He hesitated at the door. "We all missed you in school. Coach asked about you."

"He did? Well, I intend to get back into training harder than ever."

"Great. Hey, I almost forgot!" Eric dug into his gym bag. "I brought you something—it's nothing special." He seemed a little embarrassed as he handed Kelly a thick magazine.

"A *Couture!*" she exclaimed.

"I thought you might be in it. You don't already have it, do you?"

"Oh, I wouldn't be in it. Fashion layouts are done about six months before the magazine comes out. And, no, I don't have it. I really wanted this issue—it was so sweet of you to buy it for me."

Would a boy want a girl with the flu to kiss him? *Probably not*, she decided ruefully. Another golden opportunity spoiled. Instead of giving him a kiss, she just smiled at Eric.

"Well, Timmy's waiting," he said. "I guess I'd better go."

"Thanks for coming by, really."

When Eric was gone she leafed through the magazine. She hadn't been modeling long enough to be in this issue, but Paisley was. Looking at the pictures of her friend springing through the air in fabulous clothes, Kelly felt a real pang of regret, and of envy. She *didn't* want to give up modeling!

Why should one stupid mistake mean the end of the most fun she'd ever had in her life—the end of a career that was only beginning, a career that could reward her with more money than her family had ever dreamed of, enough for her to do whatever she wanted with her life.

"Don't they know how kids are?" she heard her mother saying. And, "You can't help it if you're sick," Sue had said. The excuses echoed in her head. She held a hand to her forehead, certain it would be burning with fever, but she felt cool.

"You're as sick as *I* am." Tina's voice seemed to ring out in the small room.

"I *am* sick," Kelly said fretfully, tossing the magazine off the bed and diving under the covers. "I am!"

Later that night, hearing Eric's car pull out of

the driveway, she had to make an effort not to put on jeans and a shirt and run after him. It was really ironic—because she was sick, Eric had paid her a visit and bought her a gift and nearly asked her to go out with him that night. But since she *was* sick, she couldn't go.

Maybe if she'd told Eric the truth about everything . . . well, it was too late to think about that. She tugged her warmest slippers onto her feet and padded down to the living room, plopping down with Tina in front of the TV. What a dismal way to spend Saturday night!

Twelve

"I'll get it!"

Dropping the magazine section of the Sunday newspaper on the floor, Kelly leapt off the couch and sprinted into the kitchen, beating Tina to the telephone.

"Let me get it," Tina yelled. "You're sick! It's not for you!"

"Tina, let go!"

They wrestled over the receiver.

With a deft twist of her wrist, Kelly got the phone away from her sister.

Pouting, Tina folded her arms and leaned against the wall, determined to listen if she couldn't get the phone herself. Kelly turned her back.

"Hello," she said sweetly.

"It's Alex. Haven't had a chance to call you all week. So how about brunch today?"

Kelly covered the mouthpiece. Brunch sounded wonderful. She was sick of being cooped up in the house, and if she didn't get out of her pajamas soon she'd scream.

"Brunch would be great, but . . ." She stalled, ignoring Tina's shocked look.

"I'd love to," she nearly groaned, "but I've been in bed with the flu. . . ."

"I didn't know. If you're sick—"

"Wait. I *was* sick, but really, I'm feeling tons better now."

"Did Mom say you could go out?" Tina whispered. Kelly ignored her.

"In fact, I think brunch might be exactly what I need," she finished firmly.

"Great! I thought we could go back to Ernie's. There's always someone interesting in the crowd."

She felt a pang of panic. "Uh, no one like"—she made her voice sound casual—"Meg Dorian would be there, would they?"

Alex laughed, surprised. "I've never seen her there."

"Well, then, I think it sounds terrific. I'm not dressed or anything yet."

"Take your time. I'll pick you up in an hour and a half, okay?"

Rescued! "Fantastic. See you then."

She hung up feeling very satisfied. So much for dragging through another dreary day at home—what a relief!

"You can't go out," Tina said indignantly. "You're supposed to be sick."

"Shut up, Tina. I can do anything I want."

"Kelly," her mother called from the living

room. "Did I hear something about you going out today?"

"I don't have any fever, Mom. I didn't have one yesterday, either. Really, I feel much better."

Mrs. Blake laid a cool hand on Kelly's forehead. "You do seem perkier today," she said doubtfully.

"I'm fine—getting out of the house will be good for me. I need fresh air *desperately*."

Her mother frowned. "If you go out today, it means you're well enough for school tomorrow."

She hadn't thought of that. For a second, Kelly considered crawling back into bed. But the idea of getting showered and dressed and driving to the city was too attractive. Bed no longer seemed so safe and appealing.

"It's just brunch. I have to eat, anyway, even if I'm still sick."

"Kelly . . ." her mother said warningly.

"Okay, I'm well enough to go to school, I guess."

Her father looked up from his newspaper. "You're going out? I thought you were sick."

She hurried toward the stairs. "I promise to dress warmly, okay?"

"Don't get overtired," her mother cautioned. "You know you tend to overdo things."

"I'll eat real slow," Kelly teased.

Tina tagged along as Kelly pulled open drawers and closet doors, looking for just the right thing to wear. Ernie's wasn't exactly a jeans and sweatshirt place—unless you wore the *right* jeans and sweatshirt. She wanted to look casual, but slightly outrageous.

"You sure look happy," Tina said. "I guess your flu is over, huh?"

"I think it is," Kelly said gaily. "Come on, help

me choose. The big tee top with sequins, or two plaid shirts with a big scarf at the waist?"

"For Alex? The sequins, definitely."

Impulsively, Kelly gave Tina a hug. "I'm so glad to get out of the house!"

"And with Alex," Tina said enviously. "And I guess you'll have fun at school tomorrow, too. Everyone always pays lots of attention to you when you've been out sick."

"I don't need any attention," Kelly said with some misgivings. School tomorrow was the last thing she wanted to think about. It meant explanations, and her talk to the Drama Club, and facing Jennifer . . .

"It'll be just another ordinary day," she said firmly.

If Kelly had envisioned an intimate brunch in a quiet, peaceful, Sunday atmosphere, she'd certainly been mistaken. Ernie's was every bit as crowded and noisy on a Sunday afternoon as it had been at night during the week.

"Doesn't anyone in New York ever eat at home?"

Alex pulled out a chair for her. "Not if they can help it."

The waitress left brunch menus and brought them hot coffee.

"I like that shirt," Alex said. "Those sequins are pretty funky."

"Tina picked it out. She thought you'd like it." Kelly took a sip of coffee. "Tina is one of your biggest fans."

"Someone in your family has good taste." Alex grinned.

Kelly made a face.

"Anyway, you don't look like someone who was sick."

She didn't feel at all sick anymore. "It wasn't much. One of those twenty-four hour bugs . . ."

"I hate to get sick, I hate to fall behind. I'm trying to keep my grades up this semester. There's a photography fellowship I'm after. I could quit working as an assistant if I got it."

"A fellowship? Couldn't your father pay for any classes you wanted to take?"

"Could, but won't. Anyway, winning the fellowship is a mark of distinction. I'd be taken more seriously."

Kelly nodded. "Your father still thinks photography isn't a real profession, huh?"

"He doesn't change opinions easily. You know, he wants me to study business, protect the family fortune. But, hey, we were talking about you. I didn't mean to change the subject."

"Let's not discuss me. Who wants to talk about the flu?" Taking a sip of water, Kelly glanced about casually. Suddenly she began choking, nearly spilling the entire glass of water on herself.

"Are you okay?" Alarmed, Alex sprang up.

"Don't get up," she hissed in a strange voice. "I'm okay." She dabbed at her lap with her cloth napkin.

"It went down the wrong way?"

Trying not to be too obvious, Kelly twisted her head. They were still there, not three tables away! Randy, the director from the Balmour's commercial, sitting at a table with a young girl whose glossy black hair hung to her shoulders in carefully set waves—just like Jennifer's! Kelly raised the menu so it hid her face.

"Boy, I'm starved," she declared brightly. "I can't decide what to eat!"

"Who did you see?" Alex asked curiously. "You saw someone."

"Who, me? I didn't see anyone. The omelets sound good, don't they?"

"It's that man, over there, the one with the pretty girl." Alex stared at Randy's table. "Who are they?"

"I have no idea." She began talking rapidly. "I'm just trying to decide if I want the eggs Florentine or an omelet. Maybe I'll have a plain omelet. That sauce is pretty rich, and I did just get over the flu."

Alex reached over and pulled down a corner of the menu to see her face.

"You can't hide anything from me, you know," Alex told her. "I can see right through Kelly Blake."

"You and Tina," Kelly muttered. Her face crumpled and tears welled up in her eyes.

"If you don't tell me who that is, I'm going to do something drastic!" Alex watched in alarm as she dabbed at her eyes with her napkin.

"Oh, Alex, don't!" Kelly grabbed his arm. "Please sit down."

"Not unless you tell me why you're crying."

"It's nothing, I'm not crying. I choked on my water."

"Okay." Alex pushed back his chair. "I'm going over there and ask *them* what's going on. Maybe that brunette with the big blue eyes understands you, but I sure don't."

"*Blue* eyes?" Sniffling, Kelly peered at the couple across the room. "Oh—oh, no." Suddenly she was laughing, and Alex, bewildered, gave her a look of such total confusion that she laughed even harder.

"Oh, Alex, I'm such a dope! What a terrible scare, though. I'm shaking." ·

"Kelly, what is happening? Are you laughing or crying?"

"A little of both. I thought that girl over there was Jennifer, my ex-best friend. From the back, she has the same dark hair."

"Your ex-best friend?"

"Right. But it isn't, it's an actress named Marty I met at my audition. And that man she's with is the director who worked on the Balmour's commercial."

"The commercial you shot?" Alex sat up straighter, his expression changing instantly. "That's different. You should go say hello—you'll probably work with him again. Everyone in the business knows everyone else. You should be friendly with business contacts."

"Not these contacts." She gulped down some water. "These are people to avoid."

Alex narrowed his eyes, glancing from Kelly to Randy and Marty and back again. "Let me get this straight. For some reason, your best friend is no longer your best friend, and you're avoiding the man who directed your first commercial. What's going on?"

Kelly could feel her cheeks flaming—a dead giveaway every time. Why couldn't she hide her emotions?

Across the room, Randy was playing with Marty's long dark hair as the actress gazed into his eyes.

"Let me guess," Alex mused. "If I know

you . . . you're not stupid about business. Ordinarily, you'd be friendly with your director. From the color of your cheeks, I'd guess you're embarrassed about something. I know, Randy made a pass at you and you quit the job."

"No, nothing like that."

"That girl Marty wanted your job, and *she* made a pass at Randy, and he dumped you and hired her?"

Kelly took a deep breath. "Close, but not quite."

Across the room, Randy was nibbling Marty's ear. "Alex frowned. "I hope he didn't try anything funny. I know what these guys are like. All ego and no regard for talent at all."

"No, it wasn't that, either." She took a deep breath. "But you guessed right about one thing. I did lose the job. I got fired, and it was all my fault." She told him the whole story, concluding with, "When I made fun of the script, naturally they fired me on the spot. I made the client look foolish. It was a stupid, thoughtless, unprofessional thing to do. Everyone's been making excuses for me, but I know I deserved to lose the job."

Alex was silent for a moment. "I guess you expect me to say something like, it wasn't your fault, anyone would've done the same thing." He paused. "It was a dumb thing to do," he agreed. "You asked for it."

"Great," Kelly mumbled. "Someone finally lets me take the blame."

"You probably feel better, taking responsibility."

"No, I feel rotten. Anyway, there's more. Part of the reason I got so crazed at the shoot was that

I'd promised to run in a track meet that same day. Naturally, the shoot ran overtime. I should never have promised to run that day."

"You set yourself up, all right," Alex said. "One way or another, you were going to let someone down. But how does your friend Jennifer fit into all this?"

"That's the worst part. I thought Jennifer got my part in the commercial. That's why I flipped out when I saw Marty. I thought she was Jennifer. I haven't seen Jennifer since she stabbed me in the back."

"Jennifer isn't a model or an actress, is she?"

"No, but she could be discovered on the spot. She's pretty enough to be a model."

"But can she act? Could she do a better job than you could?"

"I don't know, Alex. Right now I'd say it looks like Marty got the part instead of me or Jennifer."

"You mean you haven't talked to Jennifer? You didn't ask her about it?"

Suddenly ashamed, Kelly could only shrug. "I know it sounds crazy. We've been best friends for years and I've always trusted Jennifer. But that's why it hurt so much when I thought she'd been a traitor. I've refused to speak to her since then. She saw the most humiliating moment of my life—the end of my career—and instead of helping, she tried to take my job away! I'll never forgive her for that."

"Kelly, it is a bit unrealistic to think they'd use a totally inexperienced girl in their commercial."

Kelly squirmed. "Oh, no, it's not. I was discovered overnight."

"This is the nuttiest story I ever heard. So you thought your best friend took your job, you missed your track meet, and then you got the flu."

"Well, not really. I mean, I felt sick about everything, but I didn't ever really have the flu. I just couldn't face anyone. Not the coach or my team . . . And Meg Dorian has been calling from the agency and I haven't had the nerve to talk to her, either. Until today, I've been hiding out in my room."

Alex whistled. "When you mess up, you mess up royally. So everyone's mad at you."

"And there's more. To top it all off, I'm supposed to give a big talk to the Drama Club tomorrow about acting in TV commercials. I can't possibly confess I got fired. Tell me how to get out of that one."

It was Alex's turn to sigh.

"I know," Kelly said. "It's my own fault. Another terrible predicament, specialty of Kelly Blake. How do I get myself into these things?"

At least the worst was over. She'd confessed everything, and Alex was still there. He hadn't said she was a terrible person, and he hadn't left, either. It almost gave her courage.

"I tell you, Alex, I've done everything wrong this week. I don't think things could get any worse."

Alex threw down his napkin decisively. "First, you've got to face Meg. You have to straighten out your career."

"Don't make me laugh. My career is over. You know, it's really funny how things have worked out. I never even dreamed of a modeling career, then I got one, and now I've blown it."

Alex was grinning at her.

"What are you smiling at? Don't you take this seriously?"

"I do. It's just that I'm happy you told me all this. We're getting to be pretty good friends, aren't we?"

"Oh, don't start on that," she warned. "I'm in no mood to discuss our nonromance. I have enough trouble with Eric . . . Oops. Sorry." She colored furiously. "I didn't mean to bring that up."

"Eric—the guy across the street, my competition?"

She shrugged helplessly. "Yes. Even though he has another girlfriend, I still like him. I'm a fool, I know."

"I still like you, so that makes two fools," Alex quipped.

"Oh, Alex, you're so nice to me, I'd never hurt your feelings on purpose." She reached across the table and grabbed his hand. "I'm just messing up everything lately!"

"I'm not upset," he insisted. "We've been through this before. But, I'd be glad if you got this Eric out of your system. He can't offer you what I can; he's just a high-school kid. Maybe it seems romantic to you now because he's something you can't have." He laughed. "Maybe I should play hard to get. But I already told you—I think we're good together, Kelly. We can be totally honest with each other. For instance, you told me the truth about getting fired, but you didn't tell Eric, did you?"

"I wanted to," she said, confused.

"But you didn't." Alex leaned back, taking his hand away. "You'll come around," he said. "It's just a matter of time." He tried to make it a definite statement, but Kelly heard the way his voice caught in his throat. So he wasn't *completely* sure of himself—or of her.

She smiled. "You *are* a good friend," she said gratefully. She bent over to kiss his cheek, but Alex turned his head, catching the kiss on the lips. She was startled, and a little breathless, while it lasted. But then she remembered where they were and pulled away, blushing.

Alex laughed. "Sometimes you're so adorable. I can't wait to see you when you grow up."

"And sometimes, Alex Hawkins, you make me furious! I *am* grown up, as grown up as you."

"Not quite . . . but you're still a special person, and you'll be grown up as soon as you straighten out all the misunderstandings."

"Then don't hold your breath, Alex. I can't straighten them out. This time I'm in too deep."

It was nearly dinnertime when they finally headed back to New Jersey. As they turned into Kelly's block, Alex slowed down, then gunned the motor. Kelly shook her head when the car blasted off from the corner with a ferocious roar.

"You were right," she yelled above the noise, enjoying herself. "You *are* a show-off!"

Her father, outside raking the last of the fallen leaves into garbage bags, grinned indulgently as Alex screeched to a halt at the curb.

"That car is a beauty," Mr. Blake said, opening Kelly's door.

"Dad, don't encourage him!" Kelly pretended to be shocked as she hopped out of the car. "You're a police officer!"

Her father thumped the sports car on the roof. "Sounds a little tinny," he joked. "Did you wind this toy up today?"

Alex laughed easily. "Want to try her out, Mr. Blake?"

Her father's eyes lit up when Alex slid over into the passenger seat, tossing him the keys.

"Kelly, better stand back." Jokingly, her father gunned the motor as loudly as Alex had as he put the car in gear. "They teach us some fancy driving at the police academy," he yelled over the noise. Then he pulled out, smoothly and expertly, took a neat turn at the corner, and disappeared. Ten minutes later, when he drove back down Elmhurst Lane, he pulled the car in expertly in front of the house, stopping on a dime.

He and Alex got out. They were admiring the car together and laughing like old friends, when a somewhat battered station wagon pulled into the driveway across the street. The Powers family had returned from Timmy's special scout meet.

Eric was looking out the rear window as the car pulled into the driveway. There was no way he could have missed the scene.

Kelly's heart sank. *Great—yesterday I told Eric I was too sick to go out with him, and now he sees me all dressed up, obviously back from a date with Alex!*

She tried to act as if nothing were wrong, but one glance at Alex told her he had seen everything.

"Are you all right?" he asked as her father walked back to the house.

"Of course I am. What a silly thing to say."

"You don't care about . . . the competition?" He nodded in the direction of Eric's house.

"I had a beautiful day, Alex. Nothing could spoil it," she said bravely.

"Well, then, I'd better get going—before I

overstay my welcome." He got into his car and gunned the motor a few times, coaxing a smile out of Kelly.

"Take it easy on the highway," she ordered. "Not every cop is as understanding as my dad."

"Your wish is my command." With unusual caution, Alex pulled the car away from the curb, driving slowly up the street. As he turned the corner, he waved, and Kelly began to wave back when she realized Eric might be watching. Guiltily, she lowered her hand, hoping Alex could see her smile instead.

Why were things so complicated? Why, after years of longing and hoping for a boyfriend, was she suddenly presented with two boys who caused her so much anxiety? It was impossible to be fair to both of them, no matter what she did.

Kelly Blake, she told herself, *you have a knack for trouble.*

Thirteen

The giant red letters screamed:

Meet the Balmour's Girl: Kelly Blake tells how to be a successful TV commercial actress!

Kelly ripped the poster off the wall. That made four of them, and it was still early. She decided to check into her homeroom and ask to be excused for the rest of the period. If she hurried, she could get most of the posters down before her first-period class.

Mrs. Belvedere, Kelly's homeroom teacher, was alone in the classroom. She was surprisingly agreeable when Kelly explained that she had to help with the posters for her Drama Club talk. *Good thing I didn't say I was going to "help" destroy them,* Kelly thought, heading toward the front office. She had seen another poster there.

Julie Higgins came out of the office, holding a roll of tape and at least two dozen more posters.

"Kelly, what are you doing? Taking down the posters!" She stared in disbelief.

"Julie! I—I think we have to cancel my talk. I'm still sick, sore throat." She made her voice raspy. "I can hardly talk."

"Are you crazy? You can't back out now. Everyone in the school is coming, even the teachers! This is the biggest event I've organized yet."

"Yes, but I can't do it today. You see—"

"Just a minute. I thought we were friends, and a friend wouldn't do this to me. Everyone in school knows I organized this event. You'll put me in a bad position, very bad."

"You? What about me? I'm endangering my health."

Julie glared at Kelly in disgust. "Blake, I told you, everyone knows I organized this talk. So get it through your head, sick or not, you're speaking today. Pull out now, and you're finished socially in this high school!"

With a sinking feeling, Kelly watched Julie smack another poster on the wall to replace the one Kelly had just torn down.

Finished socially . . . Julie had the power to do it, too. Maybe people like Lisa and Rochelle would stick by her, but other kids in school would follow Julie's lead. Kelly would be shunned, left out of everything. It wasn't a pleasant thought.

Things didn't improve during the rest of the day, either. Julie had been right: everyone was going to her Drama Club talk. In Problems of Democracy, Miss Marcus made a big announcement about it, and in her last period class, English, Miss Paterson made a point of telling

Kelly she would be there, too. When the last bell finally rang, Kelly was a wreck.

"Don't be nervous," Miss Paterson said pleasantly. "I'm sure you'll get a warm reception no matter what you say."

Warm reception. Ha! People will probably throw things at me when they find out I'm a fraud. The Balmour's Girl—for about one minute.

Her stomach in a knot and her knees weak, Kelly walked toward the auditorium.

"See you soon, Kelly. . . . Can't wait to hear your talk," kids called as she passed them.

"Hey, Kelly!" A whole crew of freshman girls surged toward her. "I can't wait to find out the secret of becoming an actress," one of them gushed.

"There *is* no secret," Kelly protested, but the girls giggled and hurried past her into the auditorium. Kelly stared after them, the knot in her stomach twisting tighter. Disgrace was certain. The only blessing was that she and Jennifer had no classes together on Monday. Getting out of homeroom had postponed what Kelly was dreading most—confronting Jennifer.

She wondered what Jennifer was up to. *Apparently she hasn't yet told anyone in school that I was fired*, Kelly thought. *Or, has she?*

"Hey, Kelly! Wake up!" Rochelle and Lisa were standing in front of her. "We've been watching for you," Rochelle added, slipping a gold bangle bracelet off her wrist and holding it out to Kelly. "Here, this is my lucky bracelet. I tried to get it to you all day, but you've been in a cloud. I'd almost think you were avoiding everyone."

"Oh, thanks, Rochelle." Kelly looked at their

familiar faces. *Do they know? If I confessed now that I'm a fraud, would they help me?*

"The place is packed," Lisa exclaimed, "a full house. I'm so proud of you, Kelly."

"Our first great TV actress," Rochelle said. "I can't wait to hear you. Break a leg, that's what they say in show biz, huh?"

"Yeah, that's what they say," Kelly answered, studying their faces.

Lisa and Rochelle exchanged a puzzled look. "You don't seem very excited. Are you still sick or something?"

"Sure, it's the flu. And nerves, I guess."

"Oh, you'll be great. And we'll be right out front in the first row, so look at us if you need moral support. We'll be your cheering squad."

Firing squad would be more like it. "Thanks, see you guys later."

As Rochelle and Lisa went inside, Julie Higgins and Patty Berg appeared at the stage door with Barbara Brandon, the Drama Club's faculty adviser. "Miss B," as the students called her, grabbed Kelly's arm.

"There you are. We were all supposed to meet in my classroom, did you forget? Never mind now, just come with me." She dragged Kelly into the wings backstage. "I'll give a brief introduction, and then you just come out and talk. That's all there is to it. Now take three deep breaths and relax."

Miss B disappeared in front of the curtain. A roar of voices and applause rose when the expectant crowd saw her.

Kelly's stomach now was knotting and unknotting. She thought about Alex saying she would be a really special person as soon as she grew up and faced her responsibilities. Responsibilities! Confessing you were a phony had nothing to do with being responsible!

Miss B finished her introductory speech. ". . . So now let me introduce our very own, brand-new expert on acting for television, Kelly Blake!"

This is it. I'm going to die. No career, no friends, public humiliation . . . the end.

"Thank you, Miss B." Kelly nearly fainted when she saw the size of the crowd. With difficulty, she cleared her throat.

"Umm, making a TV commercial is not what you might expect it to be." Her throat *was* raspy. She forced the words out and the microphone screeched. The crowd stirred restlessly, and she could hardly blame them. Her voice was flat, dead sounding. But she could hardly be enthused about her own public execution.

"Uh, actually, I'm no expert on acting for TV, or anything else." She took a deep breath and shut her eyes, already imagining the boos and catcalls to come. "Actually, my experience was, uh . . ."

"Wait, wait for me!"

Jennifer bounded toward the stage, waving her notebook wildly. Kelly glanced at Lisa and Rochelle, but they seemed as surprised as she was. In the wings, Julie nodded knowingly.

What's going on? Kelly thought wildly. *What's Jennifer up to? Is this some sort of plot to completely humiliate me? Did they plan all along to expose me in front of the whole school? Jennifer and Julie and Patty? How could Jennifer go along with them! This is too much. . . .*

Jennifer clambered up the stage steps, and

Kelly covered the microphone. "Don't you dare say anything, I'll tell them myself—"

"No, I'll tell them." With an unreadable smile, Jennifer grabbed the microphone from Kelly's hand.

Kelly's heart was pounding. *I'm too young for a heart attack. But if I collapse now, I won't have to face anyone, and people will feel sorry that I died young . . .*

"Hi, everybody. Gee, there are a lot of you out there!" Laughter greeted Jennifer's remark.

"I went along when Kelly made her first TV commercial. Kelly knew she'd have to concentrate on the acting, so we decided I would take notes. Then each of us could tell you what it was like, from two different points of view: that of the actress and that of an impartial observer. And believe me, from this observer's point of view, making a commercial is no picnic."

The crowd was paying attention now. Jennifer smiled encouragingly at Kelly, who was staring at the floor. Then she launched into a description of the reality of shooting a TV commercial.

". . . It really is tedious, and difficult, when they stop every other minute to take light-meter readings or measure the focal length or adjust the sound levels. The actress is lucky if she gets two full minutes of acting in before someone yells 'Cut!' Kelly, as a first timer, was wonderful. She could really turn the acting on and off, which is probably the hardest part of the job."

I don't get it. She's been talking for fifteen minutes. When is she going to tell them?

"Are there any questions?"

"How did Kelly get the part in the first place?"

"Kelly, you'd better take over from here."

Kelly explained about the audition, and then answered questions about makeup and wardrobe, the personnel involved in production, and how much money in residuals a top commercial could generate.

As usual, Jennifer's notes were organized and efficient, and between them Kelly and Jennifer had an answer for everyone. Miss B seemed very impressed, but some of the kids looked disappointed.

"It doesn't sound very glamorous," one girl called out.

"I'll answer that," Jennifer said. "It *isn't* glamorous, it's just hard work. An actress in television commercials is a craftsman and a technician, like any other skilled worker. But she also needs talent, and you have to be born with that. Kelly is lucky because she's both skilled and talented. She's a real pro."

Jennifer smiled at her and Kelly could only stare helplessly. Was this the back-stabbing traitor she'd avoided all weekend?

Patty Berg raised her hand. "When will the Balmour's ads go on the air?"

It was the question Kelly had been dreading the most. Her mouth went dry, her tongue turned to cardboard. *Hardly the reaction of someone born with acting talent,* she thought.

"That's the worst part," Jennifer said gaily before Kelly could reply. "Putting up with the sponsors' whims is terrible! You're never sure whether or not a spot will air. You see, TV is advertising, and advertising is one of the most changeable businesses. Clients and producers are arguing even as you shoot. The Balmour's people were like that. They didn't care as much about the commercial as they did about their own egos. And it would be a real tragedy if Kelly's spot didn't get shown because of some stupid infighting. Kelly's probably the most talented Balmour's Girl they've ever had. But"—she shrugged extravagantly—"it's not a particularly logical business. Wouldn't you agree, Kelly?"

"Yes—yes, that's absolutely true. In fact, I had brunch in the city yesterday and there was my director, obviously on a date, with one of the actresses who'd competed for my part. I wouldn't be surprised if she ended up on the air instead of me. But that's the reality of show business!"

There was a lot of applause, and Miss B hurried onstage to thank Kelly and Jennifer for their talk. Kelly practically ran off the stage, relieved that the ordeal was over.

Julie and Patty were waiting for her in the wings. "You expect me to buy that story?" Julie said snidely. "The director dating another actress?"

"It happens to be true," Kelly declared. "And the friend who was with me yesterday would be glad to come and give another speech about it."

"Oh, Julie, don't be so naive," Jennifer said. "You've never been near a production house or a soundstage in your life. Only amateurs think the business is glamorous. If you weren't going to believe what Kelly said, you shouldn't have asked her to speak in the first place."

Linking arms, Jennifer pulled Kelly down the corridor, away from the crowd streaming from the auditorium.

Gently, Kelly withdrew her arm from Jennifer's. "I don't get it. Why did you save me like that? I thought you hated me."

"Hated you? I thought you hated me. Kelly, why did you run away from me at the shoot? Didn't you hear me calling? I tried to catch you before you left."

"What for? To rub it in, to tell me you were offered the job I lost?"

"You don't honestly believe I got your part, do you?"

"Didn't they consider you?" Kelly looked down at Rochelle's good-luck bracelet.

Jennifer shook her head. "Am I a model? Am I an actress?"

"They seemed to think so."

"No one was serious about using me. They were just upset and I happened to be there."

"What about the way you acted?" Kelly said. "As if you knew everything, could do everything better than me."

Jennifer looked down at her hands. "You know how I am, Kelly. I'm a perfectionist. I just wanted to make a good impression on everyone."

"You did."

"I had to. It's sort of humiliating to tag after you, to be a nobody all the time. I only wanted to be a little important myself, a little bit special."

"You? You've been special all your life. You've been the smartest, and the best dressed, the neatest—"

"Stop it." Jennifer held her hands over her ears. "Those things are so boring! I'm sick of being practical and well-organized and smart."

"But why? Jen, you're so accomplished. I always felt like a nothing around you. I was so ordinary, and you were the best at everything, and pretty, too."

"Oh, I know, I'm exotic because I'm Chinese."

"Jen, you *are* pretty. You always knock yourself and I've never known why."

"Because I've always wanted to be more like you."

"I can't believe it," Kelly said simply. "I always wanted to be more like you."

They stared at each other, and then Jennifer began to laugh. "What a pair," she finally said. "We've both been acting pretty silly."

"Jen, please forgive me." Kelly hugged her. "I thought the most terrible things about you!"

"You haven't exactly been my favorite person lately," Jennifer admitted. "I thought you didn't care about me anymore because I wasn't important enough. When Julie started acting friendly, I thought you were going to dump me."

"Thanks a lot. I hope I'm not that bad a friend. What a joke that turned out to be. I'm sorry I thought you would take my part away."

"Well, it was tempting," Jennifer confessed. "I mean, who doesn't have a secret dream of being discovered. But I know I'm not star material. And I take the world's worst photographs."

"You do not," Kelly protested loyally. "And you're the best friend anyone ever had! You saved my reputation."

"Well, I knew what you were probably thinking—that I got your part. It was the least I could do." Jennifer shrugged.

"Thanks. And Jen, you don't have to worry anymore about us not spending much time together. I have a feeling I'll have lots of free time from now on. I won't be modeling anymore."

"Not modeling?" Jennifer shook her head angrily. "Are you crazy? Of course you're going to model."

"But I can't. I can't ever face Meg Dorian after what I did! She'd never take me back, Jen."

"That may be true," Jennifer said slowly, "but you'll never know unless you try. The old Kelly Blake would've tried."

"I don't even know how to begin," Kelly cried.

"There's only one place to start."

Fourteen

It was business as usual at the FLASH! agency when Kelly arrived there after school on Tuesday. Phones rang, a steady stream of young men and women poured through the reception area and into the offices, and a swarm of hopefuls with brand-new portfolios clustered in the waiting room, hoping for the miracle of instant stardom.

Oblivious to everything, Kelly pushed her way past the receptionist's desk, anxious to take care of her unfinished business before her nerve ran out.

Nina, her booker, looked up in pleased surprise as Kelly hurried past.

"Kelly, slow down, girl! Great to see you. All better now?" The phone rang insistently, and Nina motioned for Kelly to wait while she tended to the call.

"Tomorrow, all day . . . catalog rate, not by

hourly fee . . . athletic, spunky . . . Hold on, please." On the desk in front of Nina was a circular file holding numerous cards, each listing the name and statistics of a FLASH! model. With the phone cradled on her shoulder, Nina began leafing through the cards. Suddenly she stopped. "What am I doing?" Lifting the receiver, she glanced at Kelly.

"Athletic, spunky—I think I have the perfect girl right here!" She turned. "How about it, Kelly? Can you get off school tomorrow for a catalog job?"

Kelly stared in surprise. "Me? Me do a job for FLASH!?" Nina mustn't know what had happened. Meg had probably gotten so angry she'd wiped all memory of Kelly Blake from her mind and refused to discuss what Kelly had done with the staff. Kelly took a deep breath.

"B-better not assign me," she stuttered. "Maybe you'd better talk to Meg first." Impulsively, she grabbed Nina's hand, pumping it up and down. "But thank you, Nina, thanks for *everything*. You were great to me. I'll—I'll always remember it. Well, wish me luck."

Leaving Nina staring in bewilderment, Kelly strode purposefully to Meg's office door.

At the door Kelly paused to gather courage. What had Alex said? She'd feel better once she admitted the truth. Guilt was a terrible thing. *Well*, she thought, taking one last deep breath, *so long, modeling career*. It had been short and sweet. Now it was time to face the music.

She knocked and entered.

The sunlight was so strong it was difficult to see Meg's face, thrown into shadow as she spoke forcefully into the telephone.

"I said by Thursday and I meant it—" Meg broke off when she recognized Kelly.

Kelly wished she could read Meg's expression. Maybe there was still a chance to run. But Meg was already motioning to her. "I'll be off in a minute," she whispered, covering the phone.

Restlessly, Kelly examined the office; the scene of power, of instant deals. She remembered how thrilling it had been signing her first contract in this very room. She wouldn't be coming here anymore.

Meg hung up the phone, pausing briefly before leaning back in her chair. "Well?" It was hard to tell what her tone was—impatient, angry, or simply preoccupied.

She's not going to make it easy on me, Kelly realized. "Well . . . I'm not sick anymore," she said brightly.

"I see that," Meg said gently. Her careful manner made Kelly more nervous than if Meg had exploded, the way her mother did when Kelly had tried her patience or done something wrong.

"I guess you heard about the Balmour's shoot . . ." Her voice trailed off, but still Meg made no sign of taking part in the conversation. Kelly squirmed; despite everything, she wished she could've brought a friend along for moral support—but if Paisley was right, that wasn't such a good idea, even if Jennifer's presence at the Balmour's shoot *had* saved her skin. Anyway, it was better that no one see this final scene of dismissal and disgrace.

What should she say next? She flushed, feeling suddenly warm. Her throat seemed to close. Meg was being cruel.

"Kelly," Meg finally spoke, "I think I can save us both precious time. I know what you're going to say. You're going to tell me that what happened was a fluke, a mistake. You're going to give me a million excuses and swear up and down it will never happen again . . ."

"No, no, I wasn't at all," Kelly said. She swallowed, ignoring Meg's look of disbelief. She had to get it said before she lost her nerve.

"I know it was my fault. I blew it—I opened my big mouth and said the wrong thing at the wrong time."

Meg was taken back. "Well, I am surprised," she said. "It's unusual for someone, anyone, to admit they're wrong to my face, not try to weasel out of it."

Kelly felt a glimmer of hope. Maybe Meg would be easy on her.

"But that doesn't alter the situation," Meg continued. "When you leave this office for a job, you're a representative of the FLASH! agency, not just a model out working for herself. Do you understand me?"

Kelly sagged in defeat—she was going to get the full treatment after all. She winced. "I understand," she mumbled dutifully.

"You're an ambassador—spreading goodwill for FLASH! by the thorough and competent and professional way you do your job."

"I know . . ."

"Childish tantrums have no place in any business. No client expects or deserves to put up with the kind of behavior you showed last week at the Balmour's shoot. You acted, well, like a brat."

Kelly muttered something unintelligible.

"I don't have to tell you how disappointed I am. Naturally, they've gone to another modeling agency for a replacement. It's a lucrative contract, or would have been, for you and me. You lost me money, and I don't like to lose money. I'm not in business to go broke, to give jobs away."

Kelly made a helpless gesture. "I said I was sorry," she mumbled.

"Sorry doesn't help, does it? One can only prove 'sorry' with actions, not words. What should I do with you, Kelly? Do I trust you again? Do I let myself believe you have the maturity, the good sense, to take a job and complete it, no matter how you feel about it?"

"It was the circumstances," Kelly said, hating herself for making excuses. "Really, Meg—I was working really hard. I knew my lines . . ."

"Yes, I heard all about your lines."

"I guess they told you everything."

"Actually, I made many phone calls about you last week. Conciliatory phone calls to Three Doves, to the Balmour's people, to their advertising agency; phone calls saying I regretted inferior work from one of my girls. I have to swallow my pride, too, sometimes. It's a lesson you can't learn too early, Kelly. Because every one of those people is someone I've worked with before, and would like to work with again."

"Customer relations," Kelly muttered.

"That's right. Don't ever forget this is a business, Kelly. And what's the first rule of business?"

"The customer is always right," they recited in unison.

"But what if they *aren't* acting within reason?" Kelly complained. "What if babies are spitting up on you and their mothers are fussing and complaining and you've been doing your best and you only mean to lighten things up a little . . ."

She thought she saw a slight smile on Meg's lips, but then Meg sighed and frowned, and any trace of a smile disappeared.

"Haven't you heard one word I said, Kelly? What might seem funny in a high-school classroom is not funny to adults working hard to get a job done right and on schedule."

"You're right, of course." Kelly tried to tune out the rest of Meg's lecture. It was certainly different from the big, enthusiastic speech Meg had given her in this same office when she'd first joined FLASH!—the speech about Kelly Blake's enormous potential and how she would soon be a big star, major market. FLASH! would be behind her all the way, grooming her for success. All she had to do was learn the ropes, get some experience. Kelly stared miserably at her shoes.

When Meg paused for breath, Kelly interrupted. "So I guess I'm fired, then," she said, hoping to cut the meeting short.

"Of course—they've already hired someone else. I tell you, Kelly, I wanted to see you on television, to be identified with Balmour's. It would've been quite an achievement for a new model. We could've had any contract you wanted after that—endorsements, exclusives."

"I guess I should thank you for everything you did for me. I guess I'd better go now. Oh." She fished her blank pay-vouchers from her pocket. "These are all I had left. I thought you'd need them for your records. Well, that's that. It was mostly a good experience, working here . . ." She sighed heavily.

"Kelly," Meg said in alarm, "are you quitting FLASH!?"

"Quitting?—I thought I was fired. I assumed . . ."

Meg flung up her hands. "Kelly, Kelly—doesn't that track coach of yours ever bawl you out when you lose a game?"

Funny she should mention the coach. "Well, yes . . ."

"Do you quit the team?"

"No." She felt terribly embarrassed. "Do you mean"—she hesitated—"are you saying you're not firing me?"

Meg shook her head in despair. "I'm trying to tell you, you need to shape up. You're not fired, yet. But this is a serious warning."

Kelly felt relief mingled with mortification. She'd jumped to the wrong conclusion. But things weren't so bad after all!

"Um . . . if I'm not fired . . . Nina had a job come in just now, for someone athletic and spunky. . . ."

Meg buzzed Nina.

"Yes?"

"Kelly says you got a call for someone like her?"

Even over the intercom, Nina sounded hopeful. "Yes—athletic and spunky, a full-day catalog rate."

Meg thought for a moment. "Send Jocelyn Borland. She'll be perfect. Does she have room on her schedule?"

"Yes, she can do it," Nina said.

"Thanks, Nina." Meg looked at Kelly. "Many beautiful, talented girls work for me, Kelly. If you can't make the grade, out you go. But I think you see now how important it is to behave in a professional manner, at *all* times."

"I do," Kelly said gravely. Despite herself, she giggled. "It just sounded funny," she explained hastily. "That's what you say in a marriage ceremony—I do."

"Yes," Meg said. "A marriage is also a business contract, a partnership. I'll do my part, Kelly; just make sure you do yours. And we'll have a happy marriage."

"Well"—Kelly frowned—"in this case, I guess the honeymoon's over."

With a curious twist of her lips, Meg leaned over and began searching through a stack of papers on her desk. Kelly knew she was dismissed.

As she shut the door behind her, she thought she heard Nina's voice say "Yes?" over the intercom.

Outside in the hall, Nina, still talking, waved Kelly to a halt by her desk. Kelly had an impulse to keep going—she couldn't stand having everyone know she'd been punished like a child.

Nina had finished her conversation with Meg. "Sorry about Jocelyn," she said to Kelly. "Meg likes to make her points with a demonstration."

"Does everyone know what happened?" Kelly looked around edgily.

"Listen, don't worry about it. No one escapes Meg's wrath! And as for the Balmour's people, I'll let you in on a well-known secret. They're very difficult. They've fired more models and actresses than they've hired."

"But I do have to learn to be a little more mature." Kelly sighed.

"Oh, honey, give yourself a break. Everyone gets fired sometime, for good reasons and bad. Okay, this time you goofed. The point is, you've got a long career ahead of you."

"Do I? I mean, do you really think so?"

"Forget about Meg giving Jocelyn that job. There'll be other jobs. Anyway, you look beat," she said kindly. "Why don't you go home and get some rest?"

"Can I call you tomorrow?" Kelly asked hopefully.

"Sure. Call, maybe I'll have something for you. As soon as Meg cools down, you'll get steady work again. So don't worry. Meg seems harsh, but she's fair, and she's smart. She knows a good property when she sees one. And that means you."

I'm still a model! Ecstatic, Kelly punched the elevator button, barely noticed the long wait, and squeezed happily into the crowded car when it finally came. She was still a model! Before now, she'd never realized how much it meant to her; and this had been one crazy way to find out. *Never again,* she vowed. She'd really keep her nose clean from now on, be the perfect professional. Mature, responsible, trustworthy.

Now that she had time to think, she was a little amazed. She'd never dreamed Meg would let her stay at FLASH! Everything had worked out just fine after all. She had to tell someone . . .

She hurried to the phone booth in the lobby and dialed a familiar number.

"Hollender studio," someone answered.

"Alex Hawkins, please. . . . Alex!" she said excitedly as soon as she heard his voice. "Alex, I did it. I faced up to Meg, I took responsibility for my stupid mistake, and it was all right!"

"Tell me everything."

Breathlessly, she described the meeting, summarizing the tongue-lashing Meg had given her, but expanding on Nina's kind words of consolation. "So it's all right," she told him gratefully, "the truth worked! Alex, you're a genius. I will always come to you for my business advice from now on."

He chuckled. She could tell he was pleased. "Listen," he said, "I've got to get back. Really boring shoot," he whispered. "But we'll be done soon; can I meet you somewhere? We can celebrate."

She hesitated. She had promised herself to get back home and catch the end of track practice, maybe try to straighten things out with Eric. But if they just had a quick coffee . . . *Am I crazy? I'm always getting into trouble by not saying no.*

"Listen," she told him, "I really can't today. I ought to get to practice."

"Okay. Another time. But I'm glad you called. Speak to you soon."

When Alex hung up she stood, beaming, at the telephone. It hadn't been so hard to say no after all.

Fifteen

The team was running in the woods by the parkway again today. Anxiously, Kelly scanned the field next to the school. It was difficult to see in the dusk, but she thought she recognized Matthew Gollinger heading for the showers. Eric was much faster than Matt; if Matt had finished running, Eric must have left long before. It would be just her luck to have missed him. As she was about to leave, she spotted Eric, coming out of the woods alone. *He must have run extra distance today,* she decided.

"Eric!" she shouted and waved her arms in the air.

He really had done a rough workout; despite the cold temperature, his sweats were soaked through. They wouldn't be able to run outdoors much longer, Kelly realized. One last meet and the season would be over until spring.

"Eric," she called, running up to him, "I'm so glad you're still here." She hesitated; was he at all glad to see her? "I missed seeing you in school today and I wanted to talk to you." Actually she'd avoided him. She hadn't wanted to see him until after she'd confessed to Meg.

He was still catching his breath. "What about?" He wiped his face and neck on his jacket sleeve.

"The weekend." If she didn't look right at him, it was easier to say everything. "Well, I felt funny, about you seeing me outside on Sunday. I wanted to explain. See, Saturday night, when the kids were going to the movies, well, I really didn't feel up to anything then. But by Sunday, well, you know how it is, being home with your entire family hovering over you, I went stir crazy."

"Oh, yeah?"

"Yes, and I, well, I *had* to get out of the house. So when"—she hesitated—"when my friend Alex called, I jumped at the chance to go somewhere. Everyone else I knew was away for the day," she added at the last minute. A brilliant touch; Eric would remember having told her he'd be gone all day Sunday.

"You don't have to explain to me," he said.

"I want to, you might have wondered why I was with Alex."

He gave her a searching look. "Kelly, you don't have to tell me anything. You know how it is with me . . ."

She put her hands over her ears. "Stop," she commanded. She didn't want to hear a word about Eric's entanglements with his old girl-friend. "I have something to say," she announced.

"I have decided that honesty is my best policy. No playing games."

Eric looked around. By now, everyone else had vanished into the gym to shower and change into street clothes. "Sounds reasonable."

"I want you to know that Alex is a good friend, but he also likes me, and he can be pretty persistent."

"Fine," Eric said. "Sounds perfect. A good friend who's also rich."

"He's hardly perfect," Kelly said calmly. "He's a little spoiled sometimes and he'll do anything for excitement. He can really get carried away. Actually, I prefer a more down-to-earth, sensible type. Well"—she took the plunge—"a sensible type . . . like you." It was risky to be so blunt, but after all, it was no secret that she liked him.

"I guess I'm not the exciting playboy type," he said, but without seeming the least bit sorry. In fact, he looked pleased.

"No one wants you to be a playboy," she added hastily. Had the risk paid off? "You're conscientious and responsible. Those are good qualities to have."

They walked in silence for a while. "Want a ride home?" Eric asked. "I hate the showers here. I'll drop you."

"Great," she said. Things were going splendidly.

"I never talked to you about missing the Edison meet," Eric said as they crossed the field. "I guess it was too much, working that morning when you weren't feeling well. But I admired you for trying."

"Uh, well," she said vaguely, "you know how

those things are . . ." How could she admit she hadn't been sick?

"I heard most of your talk yesterday. It almost sounded like the commercial was a bust."

"I think it was."

"Too bad."

"Oh, I don't care. There'll be other commercials."

"You know, you have a good attitude," he said. "I guess that helps when you have such a busy schedule. You don't have much time left to get in shape for our last meet, either."

"Uh . . . I'm not sure I'll make it," she said uneasily. "I haven't run, well, since last Tuesday, that's—a week ago!" She was startled that it had been that long. "I haven't run in a week!"

"I could never go that long without running."

"I'm surprised myself. I know I could never go a week without thinking about modeling. It's hard work, but I get as much satisfaction out of doing a job right as I do out of winning a meet."

"Sounds like modeling means more to you than track right now."

She frowned. "Eric, would you think I was terrible if I gave up track? I don't know what to do about it. I love to run, the feeling of it, and I even like the competitions, although I have to admit I get sick to my stomach sometimes before a big meet."

Eric shook his head. "I can't tell you what to do, but . . ." He stopped walking and was looking at her seriously. ". . . it wouldn't be the same without you around at practice and meets."

"Really?"

"Sure, I'd miss having you there. All the guys like you. And the other girls like you; you have real team spirit. And you've turned into one of the best runners."

"I'd miss them, too," she said. "Especially Sue. But the thing is, would *you* think I was a quitter?"

"I don't know," he said evasively.

She persisted. "Tell me. Remember, honesty is the best policy."

"Honestly, I think you have a difficult choice to make, but maybe modeling is better for you right now. I know it's a big opportunity for you. Maybe you have to grab it."

His words made sense, but they left her feeling stunned. Becoming a runner was the first thing she'd ever done for herself, the first time she'd ever tried to change her life. She'd never excelled at dancing lessons, had never taken piano or voice lessons as had most of her friends.

She began to see things in a new light. Running had helped her to become more self-confident, more at ease with herself, and that had helped her to look like a model. She'd developed her self-image along with her muscles. She suddenly realized that she no longer thought of herself as a gawky adolescent. Through running, she'd become both coordinated and able to handle herself better in new situations. And although she'd truly enjoyed competing and the sense of accomplishment running gave her—plus the attention she'd gotten from her family and friends—maybe now was the time to try to find that satisfaction in her career: modeling.

"Eric," she said, startled by her sudden insight, "I think I understand something. I think I understand that, somehow, being a runner helped me become a model. And I think I'm ready to let go of running for a while. I guess I knew that eventually I'd have to make a choice."

Eric smiled at her, and impulsively, she gave him a big hug. He really was terrific! He was the best friend a girl could want, and he was so sweet, and those eyes, and that smile—everything about him was wonderful.

Eric hugged her back, and they stood with their arms loosely around each other. "If you're really all better, Kelly, maybe we could have that dinner tonight . . . the one I never bought you?"

"Sounds good," she said. "Very good."

"Hey, there's Coach," Eric said suddenly, looking over her shoulder. "Over by the gym entrance. If you want to talk to him about track, here's your chance."

"Oh, no, not now," she said. "Not when I feel this good! Come on." Grabbing Eric's arm, she ran for cover, pulling him around the side of the building, out of the coach's sight.

"Tomorrow," she yelled wildly, starting to laugh. "I'll talk to him tomorrow!"

Eric laughed, too, but pulled her to a stop. "Hold on—I think I've run enough for one day."

"And I've had enough explaining for one day," she gasped, trying to catch her breath.

It was true; facing Meg had been tough. Facing the coach would be even tougher—but at least now she knew what to say.

ABOUT THE AUTHOR

YVONNE GREENE was born in the Netherlands and emigrated to the United States as a young girl. At seventeen, she began a successful international modeling career, which she still pursues today. She has been featured on the pages of all the major American and European fashion magazines. Ms. Greene is also the author of two bestselling Sweet Dreams novels, *Little Sister* and *Cover Girl*, and *The Sweet Dreams Model's Handbook*.

Kelly Blake

If you enjoyed reading this book, there are many other series published by Bantam Books which you'll love – SWEET DREAMS, SWEET VALLEY HIGH, CAITLIN, WINNERS, COUPLES and SENIORS. With more on the way – SWEPT AWAY and SWEET VALLEY TWINS – how can you resist!

These books are all available at your local bookshop or newsagent, though should you find any difficulty in obtaining the books you would like, you can order direct from the publisher, at the address below. Also, if you would like to know more about the series, or would simply like to tell us what you think of the series, write to:

Kim Prior
Kelly Blake
Transworld Publishers Ltd.
61–63 Uxbridge Road
Ealing
London W5 5SA

To order books, please list the title(s) you would like, and send together with a cheque or postal order made payable to TRANS-WORLD PUBLISHERS LTD. Please allow the cost of the book(s) plus postage and packing charges as follows:

All orders up to a total of £5.00: 50p
All orders in excess of £5.00: Free

Please note that payment must be made in pounds sterling; other currencies are unacceptable.

(The above applies to readers in the UK and Republic of Ireland only)

If you live in Australia or New Zealand and would like more information about the series, please write to:

Sally Porter
Kelly Blake
Transworld Publishers (Aust)
Pty Ltd.
15-23 Helles Avenue
Moorebank
N.S.W. 2170
AUSTRALIA

Kiri Martin
Kelly Blake
c/o Corgi and Bantam Books
New Zealand
Cnr. Moselle and Waipareira
Avenues
Henderson
Auckland
NEW ZEALAND

TRUE LOVE! CRUSHES! BREAKUPS! MAKEUPS!

Find out what it's like to be a COUPLE

Ask your bookseller for any titles you have missed:

Coming soon . . .

COUPLES SPECIAL EDITION
SUMMER HEAT!